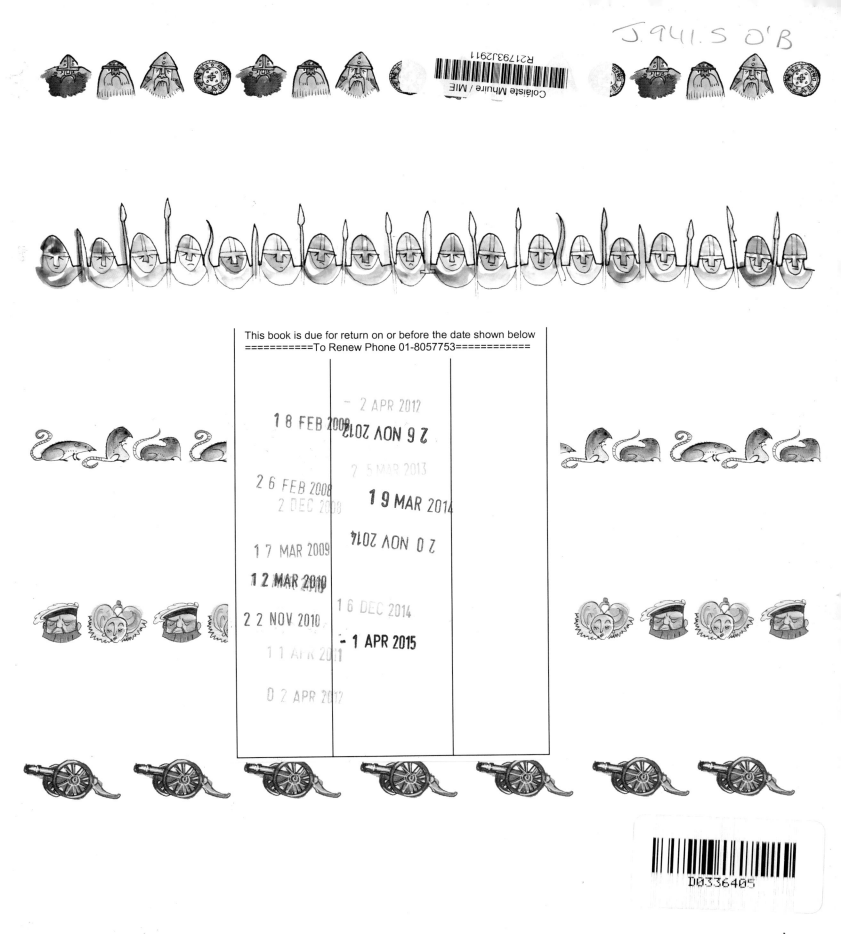

This book is due for return on or before the date shown below
===========To Renew Phone 01-8057753============

- 2 APR 2012

1 8 FEB 2008

2 6 NOV 2012

2 6 FEB 2008

2 5 MAR 2013

2 DEC 2008

1 9 MAR 2014

1 7 MAR 2009

2 0 NOV 2014

1 2 MAR 2010

1 6 DEC 2014

2 2 NOV 2010

- 1 APR 2015

1 1 APR 2011

0 2 APR 2012

The Story of Ireland

BRENDAN O'BRIEN

ILLUSTRATED BY
THE CARTOON SALOON

THE O'BRIEN PRESS
DUBLIN

First published 2007 by The O'Brien Press Ltd,
12 Terenure Road East, Rathgar, Dublin 6, Ireland.
Tel: +353 1 4923333
Fax: +353 1 4922777
E-mail: books@obrien.ie
Website: www.obrien.ie
Reprinted 2008.

ISBN: 978-0-86278-881-0
Copyright for text © Brendan O'Brien
Copyright for illustrations © The O'Brien Press Ltd

British Library Cataloguing-in-Publication Data

O'Brien, Brendan
  The story of Ireland
  1. Ireland - History - Juvenile literature
  I. Title II. Cartoon Saloon (Firm)
  941.5

2 3 4 5 6 7 8 9 10
08 09 10

Illustrations: The Cartoon Saloon:
Diane Le Feyer, Ross Stewart, Roxanne Burchartz, Nora Twomey,
Patrick Schoenmaker, Joost van den Bosch, Erik Verkerk and Paul Young.
Maps: Terry Foley, Anú Design.

Printed by Europrinting S. p. A., Milan, Italy

This publication has received support from the Heritage Council
under the 2007 Publications Grant Scheme.

AN
CHOMHAIRLE
OIDHREACHTA

THE
HERITAGE
COUNCIL

The O'Brien Press receives assistance from

the arts council
schomhairle
ealaíon

This publication has been supported by

daa
Dublin Airport Authority

helping you on your way

This Story is especially for my wonderful wife Helen and our five fine
(very big) children, Sinéad, Dylan, Donal, Sophie and Thomas.

ACKNOWLEDGEMENTS
The author wishes to thank Susan Houlden and all the folks at The O'Brien Press for their
professionalism, optimistic spirit and ambition. Along with the Cartoon Saloon they have produced a
book of a very high standard, allowing this story to be told with historical authority, humour and
warmth.

The publisher wishes to express thanks to the Dublin Airport Authority (DAA) and its CEO Declan
Collier for their substantial support towards the publication of this book. Gratitude is also due to the
following, who together with the author Brendan O'Brien, have worked tirelessly to produce a book
which will delight and inform for many years to come: Emma Byrne for her inspired design and work
above and beyond the call of duty; the illustrators who breathed life into every page: Diane Le Feyer,
Ross Stewart, Roxanne Burchartz, Nora Twomey, Patrick Schoenmaker, Joost van den Bosch, Erik Verkerk
and Paul Young; Susan Houlden for editing and picture research; Erika McGann for picture research and
production; Natasha Mac a' Bháird for eagle-eyed proofreading; Mairéad Ashe FitzGerald and Michael
Sheridan for their historical expertise and advice; Kunak McGann, Ruth Heneghan, Claire McVeigh and all
the team at The O'Brien Press for their support and administrative assistance; Terry Foley at Anú Design
for the maps, and to all those who provided the fabulous photographic images.

What's the Story?

AFTER THE ICE 4-5

AXES, COWS & PIGS 6-7

SECRETS OF THE TOMB 8-11

BRONZE & GOLD 12-3

WHO WERE THE CELTS? 14-7

SAINTS & PAGANS 18-25

IVAR THE BONELESS 26-9

THE NEW INVADERS 30-3

BLACK RATS & BLACK DEATH 34-5

ENGLAND TAKES CONTROL 36-43

ROADS & STARS 44-5

WIDE STREETS & HOVELS 46-9

SMOKING TRAINS 50-1

DEATH COMES CALLING 52-5

STATUES WITH A STORY 56-9

TO SCHOOL 60-1

A CITY IS BORN 62-3

THE HOUND OF CULAINN 64-7

FIGHTING FOR A CAUSE 68-73

IRELAND IS DIVIDED 74-7

CHANGING TIMES 78-83

ROCK 'N' ROLL 84-5

REACHING FOR THE MOON 86-9

A WHOLE NEW WORLD 90-1

FIGHTING & PEACE 92-3

THE CELTIC TIGER 94-5

AND SO THE STORY GOES ... 96

After the Ice

Our story begins 9,000 years ago when the island was a very wild, natural and beautiful place; when it had no name, no towns, no roads, no people. Of course, human beings had already been living in other places for thousands of years, but they came to this island at a time known as the Middle Stone Age.

We say 'Middle' because the Stone Age is divided into three periods: Old, Middle and New.

Our first arrivals are called Middle Stone Age people.

> The Middle Stone Age is also called **Mesolithic**, from the Greek 'meso' = middle, and 'lithos' = stone.

> Why Stone Age?
> Because we only had stone to make things like rough axes, blades, points for arrows and tiny tools called microliths.

Why did people come just then?

Because they *could* come. Until then Ireland and most of Europe was covered in solid ice like the Arctic is today. Over many thousands of years, the Ice Age ended and Ireland became a place where there was food to gather and animals to hunt.

Not only that. Ireland had become an island! Yes, during the Ice Age Ireland was joined to Britain under the solid ice. But when the ice melted, the sea rose higher and covered the landbridges with Britain. Ireland was then cut off and became an island. Some experts say the first people walked over to Ireland by wading through shallow water. But the first people probably came in flimsy boats made from animal skins. We think they crossed over at the narrowest point, coming in at the north-east corner of Ireland.

From Scotland

Mount Sandel

Imagine the Stone Age

Imagine the land which the first people saw. Imagine an island with gushing rivers and a thick covering of low-growing vegetation with fruits, nuts and berries. Brown bears, foxes, wolves and boars were roving about. In the rivers were salmon, trout and eels. In the skies, pigeons, thrushes and huge birds called caper-caillies. Everything was wild. Nothing was farmed. That's why the first people were called 'hunter-gatherers'. They hunted and gathered whatever grew naturally.

Where did the people live?

Middle Stone Age people were always on the move in search of food. They pitched their camps and hunted from there. Archaeologists have found a base camp at **Mount Sandel** in County Derry beside the River Bann, where up to 15 people lived in huts, making their stone tools and going on hunting trips.

The Middle Stone Age lasted for over 2,500 years and during this time the country became forested with oak, elm, pine and hazel. The settlers made their way up rivers, across lakes and along the coasts, spreading down to the midlands, along the east coast of Ireland and as far south as Kerry.

Late Mesolithic stone spearhead, Cloonarragh, County Roscommon.

National Museum.

Axes, Cows & Pigs

Now we are going to move on a little. Well, about 2,500 years! On to the New Stone Age. This starts about 6500BC. People were coming to the island from faraway places. Some travelled in skin boats up along the coasts of Spain and France. Others came from the Middle East and up through Europe by land.

So what was new about New Stone Age people?

They brought with them amazing new skills. They made better **stone-cutting tools**. This was a *huge change*. Best of all were their polished **stone axes**. Now, they could cut down forests and clear the land for crops.

These settlers knew about **farming**. They brought in foreign cereals like wheat and barley and foreign animals like cattle, pigs, sheep and goats to rear and eat. How is that new? People no longer had to roam about all the time searching for berries and wild food. They could **produce** food. That was really *big* – a revolution! Many of these new arrivals settled down to live and farm in one place.

Visit the **Céide Fields** in Mayo, where you can see a great farming landscape with walled fields for keeping animals in. It's the biggest New Stone Age farm-system in Europe and dates from around 3000BC.

And what's more, the New Stone Age people learned another very important skill – how to make **pottery**.

So now, for the first time, they could store things, hold water and so on.

All these changes took a *very* long time. Life changed completely.

Neolithic life at Lough Gur, County Limerick.

This is what some New Stone Age houses probably looked like.

Rock for axes

Near to Cushendall in County Antrim is a mountain called Tievebulliagh. That's where many New Stone Age people got the special rock, known as **porcellanite**, to make their polished axes, which they used to cut down trees. They also traded axes as far away as Britain.

New Stone Age is also called **Neolithic**, again from the Greek, '*neos*' = new, and '*lithos*' = stone.

Deadly secrets ... next!

Secrets of the Tomb

The New Stone Age people had no metal tools, no way of writing and yet they showed great engineering skill by heaving huge stones into complicated shapes. Five thousand years later we still don't understand what it was all about.

Tombs, tombs and more tombs

We think these people lived in simple houses of wooden posts and wickerwork. But what we know for sure is that they built amazing stone tombs to honour their dead. Today we call them **megalithic** tombs. Sometimes these tombs are called **dolmens** or giants' graves. Over 1,000 Megalithic tombs are dotted all over Ireland.

Did you know that people were buried *above* the ground in these tombs? Sometimes bodies were cremated (burnt). Most megalithic tombs were covered by a mound of earth or stones or a mix of both, like Newgrange in County Meath still is today. But generally the coverings are gone, leaving just the giant stones.

There are 4 types of tombs: **Passage tombs** (with the inner passage) are the most famous, because of Newgrange. But more **wedge tombs** have been found than any other, about 500. Most are in the south and west of Ireland. Wedge tombs are shaped large and tall at the front, low and narrow at the back. Probably the best known one is at Labbacallee in County Cork. **Portal tombs** are the simplest, like the Poulnabrone dolmen in County Clare. They have two tall stones at the front and a lower stone at the back with a massive roof stone on top. And I mean *massive!* Up to 100 tons (about the weight of a blue whale!). How did they lift them? We don't know. About 200 portal tombs have been found, mostly in the northern half of Ireland. And then there are court tombs, about 400 of them, also in northern parts. Court tombs have giant stones shaped in a semi-circle entrance leading into several burial chambers. In one, at Audleystown in County Down, the remains of 30 people were found.

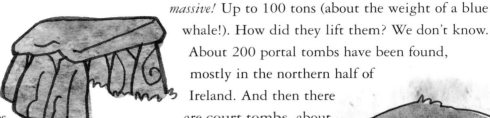

Megalithic – what does it mean? Simple. In Greek *megas* means great and *lithos* means stone.

The entrance to Knowth tomb, Boyne Valley. Some may have believed this to be the gateway to the 'Otherworld'.

What's in a name?

Poulnabrone means 'the hole of the sorrows'.

👉 Poulnabrone dolmen, the Burren, County Clare.

Do you have a Megalithic tomb near you?

If you live near Poulnabrone, you have. Poulnabrone is a portal dolmen on the Burren in County Clare (see below). There, in one tomb, the bones of 21 bodies were discovered. One was a newborn baby. Another was a man with an arrowhead stuck into his hip bone. The tomb is thought to date to around 3800BC. Wonder how that arrowhead got there? Or how the people died? We don't know. But we do know that 'grave goods' were found in the tomb, including a polished stone axe, flint-stone arrowheads and a bone pendant.

Newgrange

The megalithic tomb we know best is the **passage tomb** at Newgrange in County Meath. A dark secret is kept there. Imagine a tomb which is pitch-black for almost all of the year. You can go in through the tomb door, walk along an inner passageway but you can see nothing. And the secret? Once a year, on 21 December (the winter solstice), something extraordinary happens inside the inky depths of the passage tomb. On that day the early morning sun is at the correct angle to shine straight in the door. As the sun rises the light gradually moves inwards, lighting up more and more of the pitch-black inner passage. When the light stops it has reached, and lit up, the burial chamber in the centre, 20 metres (65$\frac{1}{2}$ feet) inside the tomb. Like eerie magic.

It's not magic, of course. These Stone Age people measured the exact angle and length of the inner passage so that the rising sun would light it up on **one day** each year. Five thousand years later it still works. And it is still a secret.

The light of the winter solstice inside Newgrange.

The mound of Newgrange.

The Screaming Stone

In legend the standing stone at Tara, the Lia Fáil, is supposed to cry out when the rightful High King of Ireland touches it.

Tara from the air. The outlines of where buildings once stood can be seen.

Newgrange is not alone

Newgrange is not alone in County Meath, where about 30 of these passage tombs have been found. A famous place in Meath is Tara. Around Tara archaeologists have found wonderful Stone Age remains, showing the area to be very important in Ireland's story. The name Tara comes from the Gaelic *'Temair'* which might mean 'A Sacred Space' or 'The Gates of the Otherworld'. We're not sure. It's a mystery.

Newgrange was built around 3200BC. That makes it older than the Great Pyramids of Egypt.

Secrets, secrets

1 Why did they build the Newgrange tomb like this?

❀ To mark the passing season?

❀ To observe the sun's 'movements'?

We don't know.

2 How did they move the huge stones into place?

We don't know.

3 What are the meanings of the carvings on the Turoe Stone, County Galway (right) and Newgrange's stones – the arcs, circles and spirals?

Again, we don't know.

What are the meanings of the swirls and carvings on the Turoe Stone, County Galway?

Next up, the Bronze Irish.

Bronze & Gold

Just imagine you are in a time machine and you are going to travel through three Bronze Ages.

A Journey through the Bronze Ages

Your journey begins about 4,500 years ago, at the start of the **Early Bronze Age**. Out the window Early Bronze Age Ireland looks sunny and calm. Something glistens in the sun. A woman, ambling along a track, is wearing a beautiful half-moon shaped necklace made of **gold**, Irish gold.

You zoom on. Then things go black. Suddenly you can't see out the window. This is the **Middle Bronze Age**.

It lasted about 500 years, but archaeologists know little about it.

On you go. Now out the window you can see the **Late Bronze Age**. It's bucketing rain. Terrible winds are swirling about. The grassy ground is flooded. But high on a hill you see a big round stone wall, like a fortress. Then another and another. Trouble. Men are fighting, firing spears down from the walls.

Bronze really changed peoples lives

When people called 'Beakers' arrived in Ireland, they brought something very new and exciting, a knowledge of metal. This was to change everything.

First there was **copper**. Copper was a metal mined from the rock at places like Mount Gabriel in County Cork. Copper was useful but it was a soft metal. By adding **tin** to the copper, people made a new type of tougher metal – **bronze**. Amazing! Pots, tools and weapons were now *much* stronger. This happened over a very long time of course. The Bronze Age ended around 600 BC.

The First 7000 Years

From Scotland

Mount Sandel
Tievebulliagh Mountain
Audleystown
Céide Fields
Newgrange
Tara
Atlantic
Dún Aonghasa
Aran Islands
Poulnabrone
Avoca
Irish Sea
Labbacallee
Mount Gabriel

© Arid Design 2007

Forest	Gold Mines	
Rivers	Court Tomb	
Lakes	Passage Tomb	
Mountains	Wedge Tomb	
Copper Mines	Portal Tomb	

1,000,000

BRONZE AGE

Ireland - population under the 200,000

Then there was gold

Remember that Irish gold? Archaeologists have found beautiful gold sun discs, earrings and spectacular gold half-moon shaped necklaces from this period. They believe County Wicklow had its own gold mine.

Sadly, during the Late Bronze Age, with the soggy, boggy weather and possibly plagues and famines, the great production of gold and bronze came to a halt.

How do you think these things were made? Mostly they were moulded. Molten hot metal was poured into shaped moulds, say the shape of a flat axe head, then cooled and hardened. Out came a metal axe head.

Gold collar, Gleninsheeen, County Clare, Late Bronze Age.

National Museum.

The preserved body of Clonycavan Man. He was murdered, perhaps in a ritual killing 2,300 years ago. He used Iron Age hair gel, made from pine resin from mainland Europe.

Hillforts

Bronze Age people needed their bronze weapons. It seems as though there was a lot of fighting going on in Ireland at this time. Remember the stone fortresses you saw on hills from your imaginary time machine? In soggy, boggy Late Bronze Age times, about 3,000 years ago? Well, they have a name: 'hillforts'. Some of these hillforts are still there! Archaeologists believe that the great fort of Dún Aonghasa on Inish Mór was started in the Late Bronze Age. These forts can be 150 metres (nearly 500 feet) across (wider than a football pitch) and often have two circular stone walls. The Bronze Age people would feel safe high on the hill as they fired bronze-headed arrows at their approaching enemies.

The Bronze Age people were right to be worried. Soon more strangers were to land on Irish shores.

Who were the Celts?

Usually when we think of the Celts, we think: blue eyes, magical, artistic, mysterious, war-like, naked spear throwers, headhunters. Headhunters! There are many myths about the Celts.

But what is the truth?

The Celts are often called 'the invisible people'. One problem is simply that the Celts didn't leave any written records, although we know something of their habits and customs from writers like the Roman emperor, Julius Caesar. Historians more or less agree that the Celts came to Ireland as small bands of warriors. In other words there was no big invasion of Celts as was once thought. These small bands made a *big* impact. They brought with them the special skills to make beautiful works of art. It's believed they spoke **Continental Celtic**, a language which is now dead and which may have started the Irish (Gaelic) language.

The first of these warriors had arrived about 600BC.

The biggest numbers came about 100BC and continued to make their mark for hundreds of years after that.

Found in the sea off Ballyshannon, County Donegal, this bronze sword hilt was probably made 100 years before Christ in Gaul (now France) and shows the link between Ireland and Europe.

National Museum.

What do we know about the Celts?

Fair hair, blue eyes

That's how Celtic leaders looked. They used to dye their hair with lime-wash, which also made it very stiff (just like gel!). Some old Latin writings tell us the Celts painted their bodies with berry-juice.

Artistic Riddles

Beautiful, curving, intricate designs were painted on leather, carved on sword handles and standing stones. But we don't know what they mean. They're like riddles.

Warriors

The Celts were warriors. Their fighting and art came together with beautifully patterned weapons and gold or bronze neck-collars called torcs.

Clothes and jewellery

The Celts (both men and women) loved to wear jewellery such as finger-rings, torcs, necklaces, ankle-rings – all made from gold, bronze and amber. Women wore linen dresses down to their ankles. Men wore the same, but only down to their knees.

Wooden houses ...

but where's the evidence?

Archaeologists believe ordinary houses were mostly made of wood, which has long since rotted away and so there is no evidence left. To feel safe, some families probably went on living in **crannógs** (man-made island settlements) which were there from earlier times. You can visit a reconstructed *crannóg* at **Craggaunowen** in County Clare (see opposite).

Ringforts (also called raths) and hillforts may have been built in Celtic times and on into Christian times. A ringfort is a circular stone or earthen enclosure, where the family lived and kept their animals safe.

What we do know for sure is how the kings and chieftains lived. You can visit the great ringfort at **Emain Macha** (Navan Fort) in Armagh, where King Conor

MacNessa lived. **Tara** was also very important to the Celts. They held ceremonies and elected their kings there. **Rathcroghan** in County Roscommon was the headquarters of the powerful queen of Connacht, Medb (Maeve)

Religious

The Celts believed that many gods watched over them, from misty mountain tops, from homes in the sky, but also from all kinds of earthly places like streams and rivers. Celtic people had **druids** to explain the mysteries of the other world. The druids were like priests, but they also acted as teachers, wizards, judges, prophets, poets, doctors and advisers to the kings; they were *very* powerful and they communicated with the gods and made sacrifices to them to keep them in a good mood.

A carved head from about 100 years after Jesus Christ, found at Drumleague, Corleck, County Cavan.

National Museum.

Merry feasts

The Celts were very fond of merry **feasts**, sitting around on animal skins at low tables. And **wine**, loads of it, was shipped in from sunny Mediterranean lands for those merry feasts.

Celtic women

Celtic women had long hair and wore long, loose, brightly-coloured dresses, dyed with juices from plants. Women could be leaders over men, though only men were members of the highest ruling groups. The famous legend *Táin Bó Cuailgne* (Cattle Raid of Cooley) tells how Queen Medb of Connacht leads an invasion of Ulster in a big battle over a brown bull.

Games, pastimes and stories

The Celts loved competitions like running, jumping and ball games. They played an early form of **hurling** and had a board-game similar to chess called *ficheall*.

Ireland has the richest tradition of Celtic stories in Europe. Many of these are about the great legendary heroes such as CúChulainn.

Naked spearmen

A Celtic spearman, it seems, wore a torc around his neck … but nothing else! He went into battle **naked**, firing spears to frighten the enemy.

Headhunters

Story-telling has it that in Celtic times the head was all important. People believed that was where the soul was.

So, often in a battle a warrior would cut off the heads of his enemies and then bring the heads to the victory feast, hanging them on poles and tent tops. There are even tales of these heads talking! Giving messages!

☞ Horse-bits from 100 or 200 years after Jesus Christ, found at Attymon, County Galway. They could have been used by Celtic warriors for their horses.

There's no doubt, Celtic times have left a huge mark on Ireland and its people. Celtic customs and beliefs mixed in with the next great chapter in the story of Ireland – Christianity.

Saints & Pagans

How did people in Ireland become Christians?

Talking to their gods

As usual we don't have all the answers from these distant times but we can be sure that Celtic Ireland sort of blended in with Christian Ireland. It didn't just suddenly happen. We know that the people of Celtic Ireland were still **pagans** hundreds of years after the birth of Jesus Christ. Pagans talked to their many gods, up in the sky, on misty mountain tops, in the rivers and so on. They didn't believe in one almighty God like the Christians.

At this time Ireland was divided into kingdoms, about 150 of them, called *tuatha*. In each *tuath* a king was all-powerful. He ruled over nobles who ruled over freemen. There were druids, certainly, who explained what the gods were saying, but no Christian priests or bishops.

Traders and raiders

By AD395 most of the Roman Empire had become Christian. The Roman Empire stretched right across Europe and included the countries nearest to Ireland: Britain and Gaul (France). The Pope in Rome was the main religious leader. He appointed priests and bishops throughout the Roman Empire. Ireland was never part of the Empire and so didn't become Christian in the same way. But people from Ireland often went in boats to Britain and Gaul. They were buying and selling things. But also they were raiding towns and villages on the coasts of Britain and Gaul, stealing all sorts of goods and bringing them back to Ireland. Many of those **traders** and **raiders** probably picked up Christian ideas and passed on the word back in Ireland.

By now Ireland had its first Christians. By AD431, we know that there were enough Irish Christians for Pope Celestine in Rome to appoint Ireland's first bishop. His name was **Palladius**. Unfortunately not a lot is written down about Palladius. He probably worked with a group of missionaries in the east and south of Ireland and converted quite a number of people to Christianity.

Ogham

Slashes and marks on stand-up stones, done hundreds of years after the first 'Celtic' invaders, may be a form of very old Gaelic writing. These are called **'Ogham Stones'**. There are about 400 Ogham Stones in Ireland, many of them in Munster.

Read the ogham stone from bottom to top: CIARA. ✳ CIARA

Which missionary made the biggest mark? Patrick

We don't know for sure when Patrick came to Ireland or how long he stayed. We think he travelled around as a missionary between AD460 and AD490, mostly in the northern half of the country.

The slave

Patrick himself told us a good deal about his Irish mission, because he wrote it all down, in the Roman language of Latin. This tells us that when he was about 16 years of age he was captured by Irish raiders and brought to Ireland, where he was sold as a slave. He had to mind flocks of sheep. Six years later he escaped, making it back to his home in Britain.

The handwritten opening of a piece from the Book of Armagh. It is believed that **St Patrick** wrote this confession, 'Ego Patricius'.

The missionary

After some more years, Patrick returned to Ireland by boat as a missionary. He toured all around the northern half of the country with groups of nobles. They preached about the story of Jesus Christ, baptised large numbers of people and set up Irish Christian churches from Louth to Galway to Donegal to Armagh and beyond. **Armagh** became the leading place in Ireland's Christian Church.

Patrick didn't make all of Ireland Christian. A lot of what happened is unknown. Many people stayed pagans, worshipping their own gods. Pagan festivals still continued. It took maybe 200 years for Christianity to spread all over Ireland.

What we can say is that Patrick was the most important of all the Irish Christian missionaries. That's why he became Ireland's **patron saint**.

Statue of St Patrick on Downpatrick Head, County Mayo, a place of pilgrimage for followers of the saint.

What happened next?

Other missionary bishops with names like Secundinus and Auxilius came in boats from Gaul (France today), converting people in the southern half of the country. They probably set up important Christian centres like Kilashee near Naas in County Kildare, Dunshaughlin in County Meath and Emly in County Tipperary.

The top of the High Cross from Monasterboice, County Louth, shows what a timber church would have looked like in early Christian Ireland.

Monasteries and churches

Ireland was changing in a very big way. Churches were tiny wooden buildings at first, but new stone churches and monasteries were built all over the landscape.

Christianity could spread in two main ways: either through monks and their monasteries or through bishops and their churches. After a while much of the Irish Christian Church was run by **abbots**, who were in charge of monasteries. You can see many monasteries, such as Glendalough and Clonmacnoise, in Ireland today. Some of these have **round towers** (which were built a little later in our story), where people found protection if they were under attack.

Spreading the word

Why does it matter who is in charge? It matters in one very important way. Soon Irish monks began leaving Ireland to spread the word of Christianity to Britain and across Europe, where warring bands of fighters called **barbarians** were attacking Christian places.

Now, instead of foreign missionaries coming to Ireland, Irish missionaries were going abroad, bringing learning to Europe during what is known as the **Dark Ages**.

Round Towers

Round towers are those tall stone towers with a pointed cone-like top. They were built inside walled monasteries. But when? It's a bit of a mystery. Historians think most were built during a three-hundred-year period from about AD950 onwards. Normally they are at least five storeys high. Each storey had a wooden floor, reached by a ladder. A large bell was probably hung from the top storey to ring when enemies were coming. The door was about 3 metres (about 10 feet) from the ground, handy for keeping those enemies out! You just pulled up the ladder! Many famous round towers are still scattered around Ireland, such as this one in Glendalough, County Wicklow.

Dark Ages

The Dark Ages began when the Roman Empire collapsed. Wild Germanic tribes attacked places all over Europe. People lived in terror. A tough new, **feudal** life took shape. These dark times lasted from about AD500 to 1100 – **600** years!

Some famous Irish missionaries

Columbanus

Some say Columbanus converted Europe back to Christianity around the year AD600. Maybe that's saying too much but Columbanus set up many new monasteries in Gaul (France). He then moved down to Italy.

Brendan

Brendan, a saintly monk from Kerry, spread the Gospel by many sea travels. The most famous was his mystical journey across the Atlantic Ocean. More on this exciting tale later!

Colum Cille

Colum Cille set up a very important monastery at Iona in Scotland. From Iona, his followers founded monasteries in Britain, such as Lindisfarne, and taught monks how to make beautiful manuscripts.

Brigid

Brigid had many followers and a special shrine in Kildare. Though much of her story may be legend, St Brigid became one of Ireland's best-loved saints and is the patron saint of spring. Her feast day is 1 February.

Hermits and beehive huts

Some monks chose a solitary life of prayer and fasting, living alone as hermits or in small groups in remote and wild places. High on the spectacular **Skellig Michael** (see photo) rocks off County Kerry you can still see some of their beehive-shaped huts, perched above the stormy Atlantic ocean.

Ireland's Golden Age

In these early Christian days, true masterpieces were being created in Ireland. Artistic people were painting and writing fabulous books, making beautiful metalwork like the brilliant silver **Ardagh Chalice**, designing gold jewellery such as the **Tara Brooch** and carving our unique **High Crosses**. This part of our story became known as **Ireland's Golden Age**.

High Cross

Ardagh Chalice

Tara Brooch

The Book of Kells

Truly famous all over the world, the Book of Kells, written in Latin on 185 skins, and decorated with jewel-like illustrations, tells the story of Jesus Christ through the four Gospels of the Bible. Not everyone agrees where it was made: either at the monastery in Iona in Scotland or in Kells in County Meath. It could have been started in Iona and finished in Kells.

Page from The Book of Kells, showing the birth of Jesus Christ.

Before we go on to meet the Vikings, let's pause our story of Ireland for the story of Brendan. We have about 1,500 years to go and Ireland is now Christian. We start to know more of what happened, because people are writing it down. Brendan's story was written quite a long time after his great sea adventures.

St Brendan and The Journey
to the Land of Paradise

Brendan was born about AD483 in Barra, near Dingle on the sea-edge of Kerry. There you'll find a mountain, **Mount Brandon,** named after him. He's famous in a lot of other places as well, because of his saintliness as a Christian monk and his sea travels around Ireland, Scotland, Wales and France.

His biggest, most famous journey was his Journey of Life.

Some think it led him to discover **America,** almost a thousand years before Christopher Columbus. On his great sea journey, he took fourteen monks with him in a wooden boat. They sailed out into the Atlantic Ocean through terrible weather, from island to island, searching for the Land of Paradise of the Saints.

It was the strangest of tales.

There was the twisting, turning **sea monster** snorting great fountains of sea spray from its nostrils ready to attack the boat when another sea creature shooting fire from its mouth arrived to kill the monster. Further on, Brendan came across the Paradise of Birds, an island choked full of birds, who could talk! One bird told Brendan that on

Sundays and holy days the birds turned into humans and sang songs of praise. Another told Brendan where his voyage would take him, saying: 'after seven years you will find the Land of Paradise of the Saints.' Elsewhere they found what looked like a smooth, slippery island, with not a stone in sight. Brendan's crew climbed on to it and lit a fire to cook a meal. Suddenly, the 'island' started heaving up and down. Yes, you've guessed it. The island was a **whale!**

In the end Brendan found the Land of Paradise of the Saints, emerging through the sea mist, a beautiful, holy, peaceful place. Brendan wanted to stay but, again, he was given directions, this time by a young man, to return home. Brendan spent his last days near Galway. He died either in the year AD577 or 583, an old, contented and saintly man, a great and famous adventurer.

Brendan's story may not be completely true, but it was written into history as a Christian message about charting life's journey and finding life's meaning.

Did you know?

If Brendan's extraordinary journey across the Atlantic were true, it would mean he reached America **900** years before Christopher Columbus! Was it even possible? Well, in 1976, one adventurer called **Tim Severin** tried for the answer. In a boat made just like the one Brendan might have used, he and a five-man crew sailed from Kerry on the same route as Brendan. Tim Severin's dangerous journey took over a **year**; but, guess what, they made it to Newfoundland in north America!

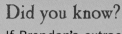 A rare photograph of Tim Severin's reconstructed St Brendan boat in action.

Ivar the Boneless

In the 'Golden Age' of early Christianity, Ireland was still divided into many tribal kingdoms. The High King was the king of all the kings, but he had only his own personal army – not one to protect the whole country. Ireland still had no towns. Monastery enclosures were safe places, and that's where many people lived. Well, as it turned out, the monasteries weren't so safe after all. Not when the Vikings arrived, from about AD800.

Hit-and-run Vikings

The Vikings were great boat-builders, sailors and fighters from Norway, Sweden and Denmark. They were pagans, not Christians. Their sleek longboats were very advanced for the time, 18 metres (60 feet) long, carrying up to 120 men. They could travel across the ocean by sail or up rivers by rowing, often arriving swiftly in surprise attacks on monasteries, where they stole valuable goods, took food, killed defenders and captured slaves.

For many years before AD800, Viking raiders had been plundering around the Irish coast in hit-and-run attacks.

But, of course the Vikings attacked other countries too, such as England, northern France, Spain and Iceland. They even reached north America's coast but were beaten back by the Native Americans.

The Vikings used Ireland's rivers like the Shannon to travel deep into the country. One story tells of 60 Viking ships on the Boyne and 60 on the Liffey. The Vikings were not always the winners. Many of them were part-time invaders, spending most of the year farming. Some Irish leaders also fought back. For instance Malachi I captured the Viking leader Turges and had him drowned!

After a while the Vikings changed their methods. Instead of just making hit-and-run attacks, they began to set up towns such as Wexford, Waterford, Cork, Limerick and Dublin, where they lived and kept control. Dublin was founded in AD841 and became their most important Irish base.

The Sea Stallion, a replica of a Viking longship. The original boat was made with wood from Glendalough, nearly 1,000 years ago, and the remains can be seen at the Viking Ship Museum, Roskilde, Denmark.

Slaves and Towns

For the next 150 years the Vikings expanded these new
towns. They lived normal lives, fought Irish kings, sailed off
to new adventures and brought back slaves and stolen goods.
At one point they were driven out of Dublin but some years
later they returned with a huge fighting force and won
Dublin back. Eventually, the Vikings were defeated at the
Battle of Tara in Meath in the year AD980 and at the Battle
of Clontarf near Dublin in AD1014 by the High King **Brian
Boru**. Some Leinster chiefs had sided with the Vikings at
Clontarf, where Brian was killed.

But it wasn't the end of the Vikings in Ireland. Viking
people stayed and mixed with the local Irish in the new
towns. Dublin was becoming an important city with its own
government, coins and trade with Britain and the
Continent.

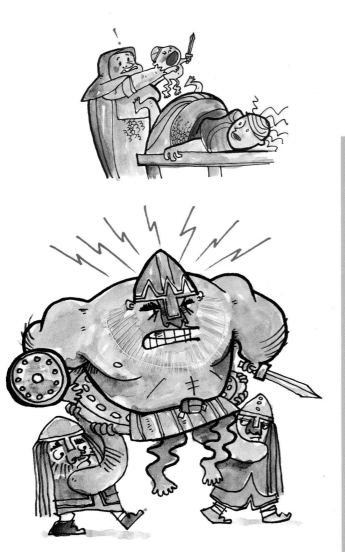

Ivar 'the Boneless'

Stories tell of how **Ivar the Boneless** was born with almost no
bones in his legs because of a curse or a disease. We hear
that he was carried on a metal shield into battle; that he was
a Viking king of great wisdom, but also a ruthless invader
with very powerful arms and upper body.

Ivar's father was king of Denmark, the famous Viking warrior
known as King Ragnarr 'Leather Breeches'. One of Ivar's
brothers had another great name. He was called Sigurd or
'Snake-Eye'.

At one point King Ivar ruled Dublin. He used Dublin as a
base to attack and plunder parts of Scotland and England,
bringing back all kinds of stolen goods and **slaves** to be sold
at Dublin markets.

Ivar died in AD873 as 'King of the Northmen of all Ireland
and Britain'. He died rich, powerful, unbeatable in battle and
still pagan.

Smelly Dublin

If you lived in Viking Dublin your *little* house would have been made from **post and wattle** (wooden posts held together with woven hazel or elm like a woven basket) with open holes for windows and an open hole in the roof for smoke from the fire. Your house would be in a row of houses and workshops – weaving, leatherwork, bonework (for making combs) and pottery all went on in Dublin.

You might have been living with your animals too: cows, horses, goats, chickens, ducks, swans, pigs, dogs and cats!

So how did all these people go to the toilet? They used big holes in the ground called **cesspits**. Hold your nose and imagine carrying your, em, stuff in a kind of bowl to dump it in the pit.

How do we know so much about Viking Dublin?

During the last part of the twentieth century, archaeologists did work near the Liffey, around Christ Church Cathedral and Temple Bar before new buildings were built there. They dug up an amazing and wonderful array of ordinary household things and the remains of houses, as well as weapons and jewellery buried with people when they died.

There were, of course, bigger houses and places where the more 'important' people lived. These people had expensive beeswax candles to give light, for instance. A lowly family made do with simple oil lamps or the sort of candles which gave off smelly smoke and gave very little light. *And* the smoke filled your eyes with pain.

With all those people and animals living together, and with the smoke and the cesspits, Dublin must have been a very smelly place.

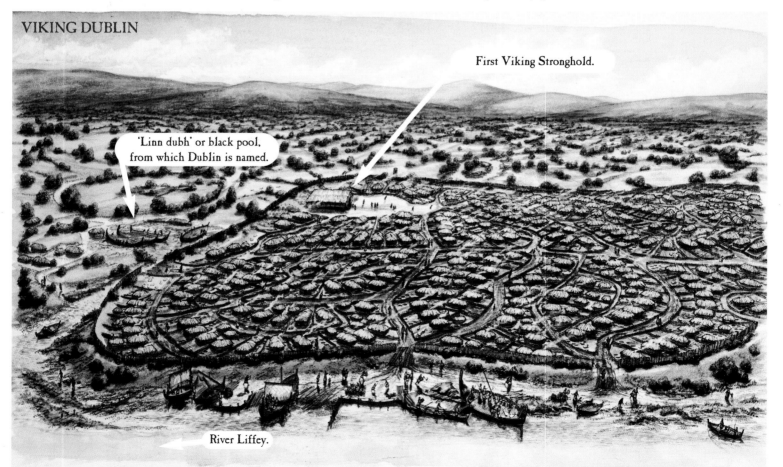

VIKING DUBLIN

First Viking Stronghold.

'Linn dubh' or black pool, from which Dublin is named.

River Liffey.

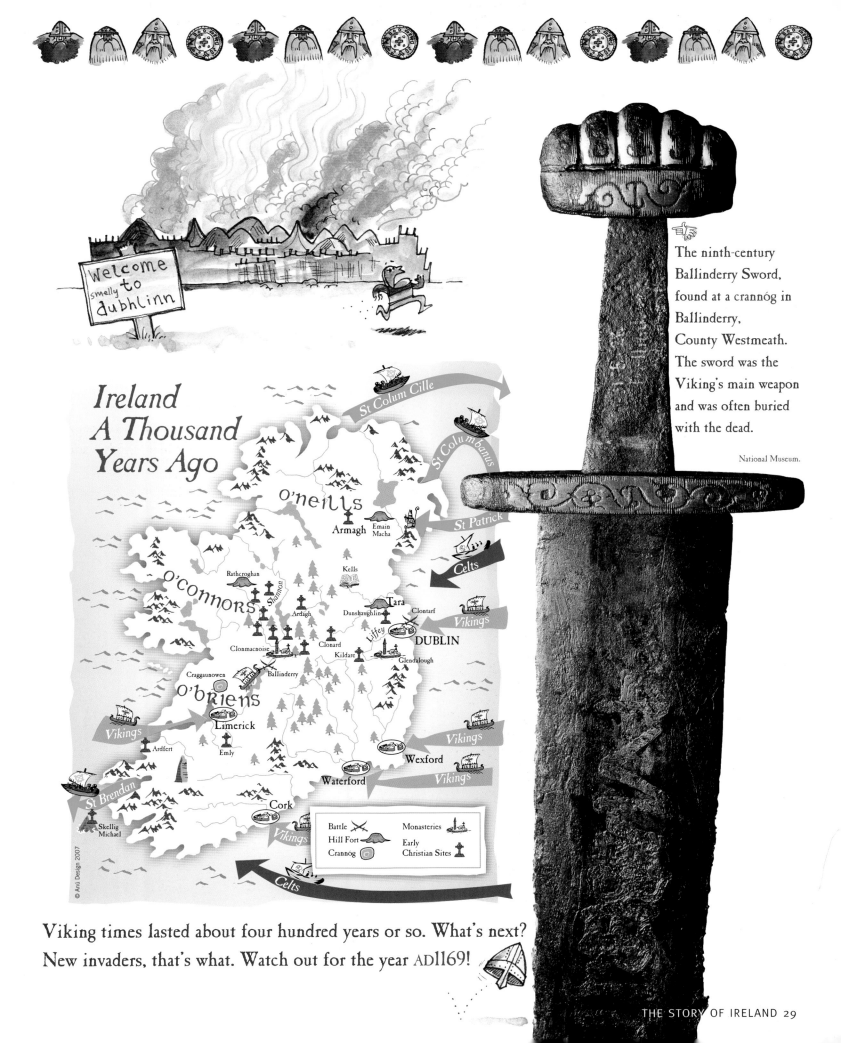

Welcome to smelly dubhlinn

The ninth-century Ballinderry Sword, found at a crannóg in Ballinderry, County Westmeath. The sword was the Viking's main weapon and was often buried with the dead.

National Museum.

Ireland A Thousand Years Ago

St Colum Cille

St Columbanus

St Patrick

Celts

Vikings

Vikings

Vikings

Vikings

Celts

St Brendan

o'neills

Armagh   Emain Macha

o'connors   Rathcroghan   Kells

Shannon   Ardagh   Tara   Clontarf
Dunshaughlin   DUBLIN
Clonmacnoise   Clonard   Liffey
Kildare   Glendalough
Craggaunowen   Ballinderry

o'briens   Limerick

Ardfert   Emly

Wexford

Waterford

Cork

Skellig Michael

© Anú Design 2007

Battle ⚔   Monasteries
Hill Fort   Early
Crannóg   Christian Sites

Viking times lasted about four hundred years or so. What's next? New invaders, that's what. Watch out for the year AD1169!

We have travelled about 8,000 years through The Story of Ireland.

By now more and more of our story is written down. We know more about it. Things are changing faster.

We have just heard about the Vikings: how they controlled the area around Dublin and the new towns of Wexford, Waterford, Cork and Limerick.

Pay up, or else!

Outside of Viking territory, Irish kings and ordinary people lived in the countryside. Many obeyed the **Brehon Laws**, where family groups had to take responsibility for the crimes of their members. For instance, if Conor O'Brien stole a horse from one of the O'Rourkes, a judge would decide a fine had to be paid to the O'Rourkes. If Conor didn't pay, another O'Brien had to pay and it was his job to get the money back from Conor. But if, in the end, robber Conor never paid up then his family would disown him and he lost all legal rights. This meant the O'Rourkes could use him as a slave or even kill him!

The Brehon Laws were considered to be fair. Usually people made agreements by their word of honour, their **Oath**. The Oath of a higher-ranking person overrode the Oath of a lower-ranking person when it came to disputes. **Land** was usually owned by the family group as a whole not by one person. **Women** had very few rights, except as wives of their husbands. When a **king** died his title didn't go to the eldest son. All his sons had a chance and usually the toughest son, or the most cunning, ended up as king!

A life-sized model of Strongbow, leader of the Norman invaders.

Dublinia exhibition, Dublin.

The last High King

For a very long time the Uí Neills (O'Neills) in the northern half of Ireland were the most powerful Irish family. Then the O'Briens of Munster took control when **Brian Boru** won many battles and became High King of Ireland, calling himself 'Emperor of the Irish'.

Even after Brian Boru was killed at the Battle of Clontarf in 1014 the O'Briens stayed on top for most of the next hundred years. But the O'Connors had something to say about that. In Connacht they were gathering strength, building castles and forming a large force of fighting ships. Eventually **Rory O'Connor** became High King in the year 1166. In fact Rory was the last High King of all Ireland. More on that later!

The new invaders

Remember that date? 1169? It's a vital year in Ireland's story. That's when the next band of invaders, the **Normans**, arrived from Wales in fighting ships at Bannow Bay off Wexford. These 'Normans' were originally from Normandy in northern France, although they had conquered much of Britain.

They were brought in by Diarmuid MacMurrough of Leinster. Diarmuid lost his title as King of Leinster when the O'Rourkes and the new High King Rory O'Connor beat him in battle. Diarmuid had hoped to become High King himself, but he was now banished from the country. One way or another, Diarmuid was looking for his title back!

He got it back when the Norman invaders came. They were led by a man nicknamed **Strongbow** (his real name was Richard fitz Gilbert) who took over most of Leinster, including Waterford and Dublin. Strongbow married Aoife, daughter of Diarmuid MacMurrough, and he even became lord of Leinster after Diarmuid died. The Normans had fighting methods that the Irish couldn't match. Their deadly weapon was the **long-bow** and they were brilliant at using it. They themselves were well protected by wearing chain mail and iron helmets.

MEDIEVAL DUBLIN, AROUND 1275

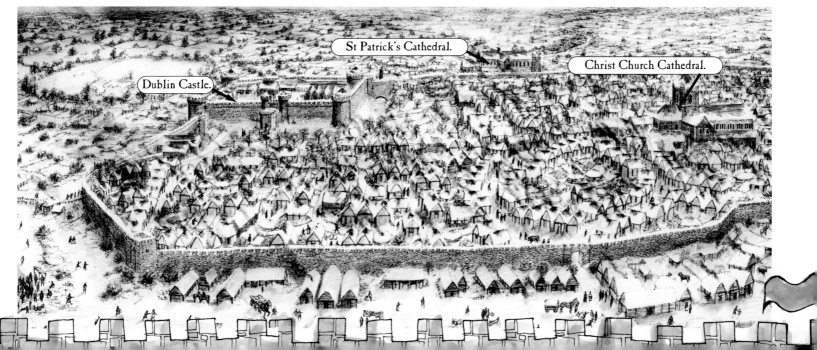

St Patrick's Cathedral.

Christ Church Cathedral.

Dublin Castle.

The Normans take control

Then came a really big move. King Henry II of England arrived with a huge fighting force in 1171. Soon almost all Ireland's kings, including Rory O'Connor, were forced to accept Henry as Lord of Ireland at a big gathering in Dublin. Rory had been the greatest and most powerful of all the high kings. Now his power weakened more and more as English-Norman control got stronger. Rory O'Connor died a broken leader at Cong in County Mayo in 1198, the last High King of Ireland.

Over the next hundred years the Normans brought really big changes to Ireland. They built a lot of very strong castles, such as Trim Castle in County Meath, started up most of Ireland's towns and eventually took over most of the best fertile land. If you could have flown over Ireland at this time you would have seen large areas of forest, lots of small villages, big open fields divided into strips, stone castles, churches and monasteries and walled towns, such as Dublin and Limerick. The Normans were master soldiers and organisers. They organised great religious orders like the Franciscans, Dominicans, Cistercians and Augustinians. They made a big mark on farming, loved music and poetry and … you might like to know … they brought rabbits to Ireland!

Rory o'Connor R.i.p 1198

Aughnanure Castle, a tower-house you can visit in County Galway.

Castles

By 1500 there were over 3,000 castles in Ireland, many of them owned by Irish chieftains. Most of them were what are known as **tower-houses**. They were built to protect the lord or chieftain and his family, so they had features like arrow slits, murder-holes (holes in the roof or passageway, through which boiling oil or rocks could be dropped on the enemy) and spiral staircases. You can visit castles such as Bunratty in County Clare, Barryscourt in County Cork and Aughnanure in County Galway to get a good idea of what they were like to live in (draughty and not very comfortable!).

The Normans were conquerors, but they also mixed with the Irish and married them. As a result of this, there's a famous saying in Irish history about the Normans: they became 'more Irish than the Irish themselves'.

Next ... the black rats!

WARNING!
Don't read this chapter with your dinner!

Blame it on the flea

The Oriental Rat Flea. He's the nice chap who got infected in his stomach. Then he sucked blood from a black rat, and the infection got into the rat's blood. Other fleas, who sucked blood from the rat, got infected too. When the rats died from infected blood, the hungry fleas had a go at human beings and … the humans got huge big bluey black bumps and lumps, aching arms and legs, and fever. They vomited terribly, spewed out slimey 'red blood' and quickly died.

The **Black Death** had begun in Ireland. It was 1348.

Actually we believe the Black Death began a long way away, maybe in China. It was spread across Europe by people running away from it in panic and by infected people spreading the disease while travelling along 'trade routes', buying and selling goods.

The Black Death wiped out whole families, whole villages and very many people in the dirty towns of the time. It's thought that about one third of all people living in Europe died from the Black Death, all within about four years!

Imagine dead bodies everywhere; people scared to bury their dead brothers and sisters, afraid they'd get infected; priests going to comfort the dying, getting infected and dying too.

The Plague
People of the time called the Black Death 'The Plague'. There were three types of plague but the most common was the **bubonic plague,** the one that gave you the big lumps.

Robert Hooke's drawing of the Oriental Rat Flea from his Micrographia of 1664.

The Black Death

The story of the Black Death in Ireland was written down in Latin by **Friar John Clynn**, who then died from the plague himself. Friar Clynn wrote his Black Death journal in a Dominican friary in Kilkenny. He said the plague arrived in Ireland through the shipping inlets of Drogheda and Howth (or Dalkey). Friar Clynn wrote:

> *'… many died from boils and ulcers and running sores which grew on the legs and beneath the armpits, whilst others suffered pains in the head and went almost into a frenzy, whilst others spat blood. There was hardly a house in which one only had died, but as a rule man and wife and the children went the common way of death.'*

People died especially in the crowded towns like 'smelly' Dublin, Cork, Waterford, Wexford and Limerick. We don't know exactly how many died in Ireland, but historians think between a third and half of the population died! We don't know for sure, but that could be as many as 400,000 dead!

We know that the Black Death changed Ireland: towns shrank; many Norman conquerors abandoned their big houses and controlled less of the country; farming just stopped in many places and, because lots of the priests died, the Church was knocked backwards.

One final thing ... we do know the plague came back on and off in later years ... ugh!

England takes Control

Our story has come to a very important time,
when we hear how England takes control of Ireland.

Stop mixing with the Irish!

If you live in Ireland today, you live in a county. It might be County Cork? Armagh? Dublin? It could be any one of the 32 counties on the island of Ireland. This is not how it was in the year 1500.

Ireland was not yet divided into counties. Many places still had strong Gaelic rulers like the O'Neills in Ulster. Around Dublin and parts of Leinster, the area known as 'The Pale', the 'Old' English-Norman lords and families ran things themselves. Having been in Ireland more than 200 years they mixed with the Gaelic Irish, married them, were entertained by their travelling minstrels and only half obeyed the king in London. Some powerful lords like the Earl of Kildare ruled almost like kings.

Way back (in 1366 in fact) the Irish parliament had passed a set of laws called the **Statutes of Kilkenny**, forbidding all this mixing and marrying, no speaking Gaelic or wearing Irish clothes or hair styles. The Statutes said these lords must defend England's territory around Dublin better. But for many more years not too much changed around the Pale.

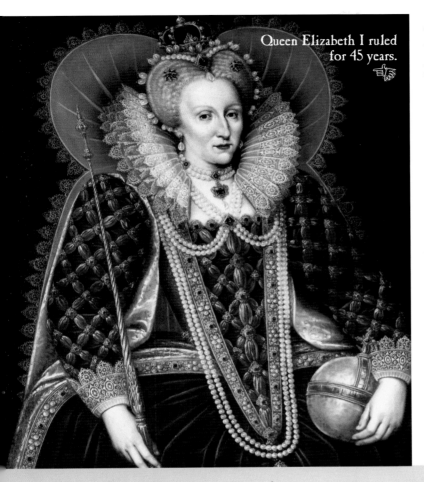

Queen Elizabeth I ruled for 45 years.

A new king and a powerful queen shake things up

Life in Ireland was to change when a new king of England, King Henry VIII, took over in the year 1509. Henry was determined to bring Ireland more under English control. Around this time in Europe the Roman Catholic Church split, in what was called the Reformation. That's when Protestantism started. In England Henry broke away from the Pope in Rome and made himself head of the Church of England. He wanted Ireland to obey him as king and head of the Church and he did away with many monasteries. Henry feared that Irish leaders might side with the Pope against him. Some supported Henry and some did not.

What's certain is that a long struggle to force English rule on all of Ireland had begun, leading to terrible war during the reign of Henry's second daughter, Queen Elizabeth I (see opposite).

 Grace O'Malley ruled the seas from Rockfleet Castle on Clew Bay, County Mayo.

Grace O'Malley (Granuaile)

At the time of Queen Elizabeth I of England, Grace O'Malley, known as the **Pirate Queen**, ruled over large areas of land around County Mayo. From her base at **Rockfleet Castle**, on Clew Bay, she also controlled the seas off the west coast of Ireland. Her ships stopped other passing ships and forced the captains to pay for safe passage into Ireland. The English tried to capture Grace O'Malley, and after many fierce attacks, they eventually succeeded in throwing the pirate queen into a dungeon jail in Dublin Castle. But Grace O'Malley demanded to see Queen Elizabeth and there was a famous meeting between these two powerful women. Grace was allowed to return home to Rockfleet Castle, to remain there for the rest of her life.

Kinsale, Christmas Eve 1601

In Ulster the Irish chieftain Hugh O'Neill had a secret plan. He was promised an army of soldiers from Spain. Between them they would finish off the English, at least in Ulster.

Then at last, in September, 3,000 Spaniards arrived, not off the north coast as Hugh O'Neill expected, but at Kinsale at the very bottom of the country. Things were not looking too good. The Spaniards were promised a lot of horses and other help from Gaelic chiefs in Munster, but not much came.

Soon thousands of English soldiers trapped the Spaniards at Kinsale.

Now Hugh O'Neill, as well as Red Hugh O'Donnell and their Ulster armies, had to trudge more than 6,000 men over mountains and flooded land in wintry weather down to Kinsale.

Even still, the Irish and the Spaniards could have won. They had many of the English soldiers sandwiched between their two armies. They could attack from both sides!

But when attack time came that dark, stormy Christmas Eve morning, signals between O'Neill's and O'Donnell's men got all mixed up. The Spanish soldiers didn't move because planned signals never came. Horses took fright in the electric storm.

In a short savage battle the English badly defeated the Irish. The Spaniards surrendered. Just a few years later the O'Neills and O'Donnells left Ireland, never to return. This is written in Ireland's story as the **Flight of the Earls**, a very big event.

🐦 Kinsale harbour, County Cork, today, showing Charles Fort, a massive, star-shaped, defensive fort, built around 1677.

Queen Elizabeth defeats the Irish

Queen Elizabeth's armies fought many battles with Irish lords, especially Hugh O'Neill in Ulster, the Earl of Tyrone. Hugh O'Neill had many successes but he was defeated at a famous battle in **Kinsale**, County Cork in the year 1601, which broke the power of the Irish chieftains for good.

Spanish ships would have made an amazing sight as they sailed around the coast of Ireland in 1601.

English control is complete

Why was the **Flight of the Earls** so important? With these big Gaelic leaders gone English rule could be spread to rebellious Ulster and other Gaelic-run areas. Soon Ulster was finally divided into counties, each run by a sheriff with English law, as other counties were. The final counties came later, making 32 in all Ireland. After Elizabeth died in 1603, King James I took even more control of Irish land.

The Ulster Irish lose their land

Remember how the O'Neills and O'Donnells abandoned Ulster after the Battle of Kinsale? You heard that the new King, James I, took even more control. This is what he did. In 1609, he started what is known as the 'Plantation of Ulster'.

Thousands of Protestant 'planters' from England and Scotland were given lands, at good prices, owned by Ulster's Catholics. Planters built new towns and castles, to keep Ulster safe for the English Crown. This divided native Catholics from the new Protestant 'planters' … storing up trouble for the future.

Ulster was not the first

The Plantation of Ulster became the best known plantation in Ireland's story but it was not the first. Already plantations had been set up in what was called Queen's County (now Laois) and King's County (now Offaly) as well as in Monaghan and in parts of Limerick, Kerry, Cork and Waterford. One famous Englishman Sir Walter Raleigh was given 42,000 acres in Munster.

Some new landowners brought valuable skills and businesses, such as new cattle breeds, or helped build towns like Derry, Belfast, Youghal and Kinsale. All the while the native Irish were fighting back on and off, including a major war in Munster, until there was one big all-out rebellion in 1641.

One of the canons from the thick walls of Derry, a town built during the Plantation.

In a darkened room

Around this time **bards** wrote a lot of poetry about the tragic things happening in Ireland. Bards were special Gaelic poets whose tradition went back a very, very long way. Bards were taught in Bardic Schools with very strict rules. Often they had to compose poems in a darkened room, by memory, and could only write them down when they came out!

Rebellion

That rebellion of 1641 began in Ulster, but in places it was very disorganised and terrible killings were carried out by Catholic rebels. In one long-remembered event in Portadown 80 Protestants were piked, shot dead or thrown off a bridge. Soon the Catholic 'Old' Norman-English of the Pale around Dublin joined in making it a countrywide Catholic rebellion lasting 12 years. In the end a new English ruler Oliver Cromwell, who had overthrown the king in London, came to Ireland and crushed the rebellion. More than 600,000 people had died in battle or from starvation and plague during those 12 terrible years. Ireland was now more bitterly divided than ever. There were big battles ahead.

Oliver Cromwell

Oliver Cromwell was a Protestant military leader in England. When he defeated and executed King Charles he became England's ruler with a plan to rule more fairly. But that is not how Cromwell is remembered in Ireland. He arrived there in August 1649 with his New Model Army of 20,000 soldiers to fight those loyal to the king. Cromwell's men carried out terrible massacres in Drogheda and Wexford. They executed or deported Catholic priests. Many Catholics were forced off good land, onto poorer land in Connacht. 'To Hell or to Connacht' is how Cromwell threatened them. Cromwell's nickname was **Ironsides**.

Remains of O'Brien's castle on Inisheer Island, County Galway, destroyed by Cromwell's men.

I want to be king!

In 1688 the then Catholic King of England, **James II**, was forced to leave the throne and a Protestant King called **William of Orange**, from Holland, was invited to be king. James came to Ireland looking for support. This led to a war in Ireland between James and William, which William won, in the year 1691.

William of Orange and hand-to-hand combat at the Battle of the Boyne.

Battle of the Boyne, 1 July 1690

We'll call this the **Battle of a Thousand Horses!**

King James arrived in Ireland with an army of French soldiers to take control. This worried England's new Protestant King, William of Orange. William sailed into Belfast Lough with a huge army and 1,000 horses in 300 ships!

On 19 June William's army began a march to Dublin. James decided to block him at the River Boyne. William arrived at the Oldbridge river crossing with 36,000 soldiers, on one side of the river. On the other side James had 25,000. Ready for battle!

In a clever move, William split his army into two sections and took James by surprise. Confused and divided, James's army found itself trapped by the river. In the end, without a lot of fighting, James and the French soldiers fled away and William easily won the day. It was 1 July 1690 (12 July by today's calendar), a famous day in Ireland's story.

The 'wild geese' who went to fight for France wore a distinctive red uniform and long-haired wig.

Limerick and the wild geese

Limerick City was the last place to hold out against King William, but in 1691 it was forced to surrender. Under an agreement called the **Treaty of Limerick** Irish soldiers left Ireland as '**wild geese**', as they were called, and went to fight for France. The Treaty said others could keep their lands and jobs and Catholics could practice their religion. In return William got peace in Ireland, leaving him free to fight his enemies in Europe.

However, Catholics did not get their promised freedom.

One rule for Protestant, one for Catholic

Soon very harsh laws known as popery laws or penal laws were brought in against Roman Catholics.

The idea was that Ireland would be controlled by people connected to the main Protestant Church, the Church of Ireland. These laws said that bishops and priests had to leave Ireland. Catholics couldn't vote, or buy land or carry weapons, or go to Catholic schools, or own a horse worth more than £5.

However, bishops and priests quietly continued. Children were educated in fields and barns in what were called **hedge schools**. Many wealthy Roman Catholics held on to their wealth and land by joining the Protestant Church of Ireland.

This has been a violent and very important time in Ireland's story. We've seen great battles and the end of the great Gaelic rulers. By the year 1700 England had certainly taken control.

After all that you deserve a pause.
It's time for travel and superstitions.

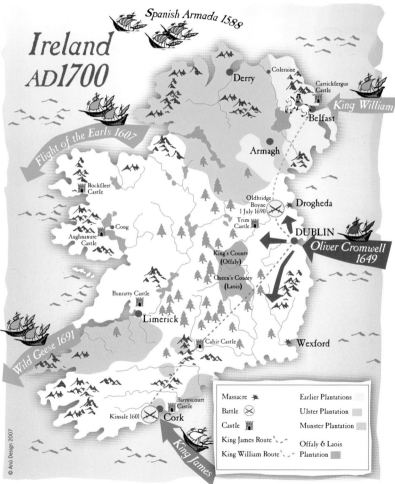

Ireland
AD 1700

Spanish Armada 1588

Flight of the Earls 1607

King William

Wild Geese 1691

Oliver Cromwell 1649

King James

Derry · Coleraine · Carrickfergus Castle · Belfast · Armagh · Rockfleet Castle · Cong · Aughnanure Castle · Oldbridge Boyne 1 July 1690 · Trim Castle · Drogheda · DUBLIN · King's County (Offaly) · Queen's County (Laois) · Bunratty Castle · Cahir Castle · Wexford · Limerick · Barryscourt Castle · Kinsale 1601 · Cork

© Arid Design 2007

Legend	
✳ Massacre	Earlier Plantations
⚔ Battle	Ulster Plantation
🏰 Castle	Munster Plantation
King James Route	Offaly & Laois
King William Route	Plantation

Roads & Stars

Very often roads get little or no mention in Ireland's story. Yet, they were pretty vital. So were stars. But what's the connection between roads and stars?

The Star of Knowledge

For a very long time when there were no cars or aeroplanes and very few clocks, people took their direction from *an réalt eolais*. In Irish this means 'the star of knowledge', known today as the **North Star**. When people faced *an réalt eolais*, they were facing north. And how did they know the **time**? They looked out for *an Tréidín*, meaning in Irish 'the little herd'. That's a little group of stars today called the **Pleiades**. The position of *an Tréidín* in the night sky gave them the time, in a similar way to the sun in the daytime.

If we go a long way back in our story, say back to the New Stone Age, we believe that roads started just as you would expect. People beat down

bushes and grass, making tracks for walking. In time the most popular trackways became highways. We know that later, by Christian times, Ireland had some fine straight highways called *Sligthi*, some paved with large timber slabs. These roads were wide enough for two horse-pulled carts to pass. Five *Sligthi* were said to have fanned out from **Tara**, the ancient centre of the high kings of Ireland.

Roads were not someone else's business. People who lived along the highways had to keep them clear of weeds, bushes and falling trees.

During Viking times roads were improved. The Vikings built new towns. Good roads were needed to travel and trade between them.

Stop lurking about!

In Norman times, English law on roads began to be applied in Ireland. One law said that roads should have clear spaces on either side so that thieves and highwaymen couldn't hide, or as the Statute (law) of Winchester said,

> ... so that there be neither dyke, tree or bush whereby man may lurk to do hurt.

Later there was the **six-day** law when each **parish** was given the job of repairing and building main roads and

bridges. In each parish men had to do road work for six days between Easter and Midsummer Day in June. But this meant that main roads became higgledypiggledy as you went from parish to parish. So things were changed, in the year 1765. Now each **county**, not parish, was responsible for main roads. These roads had to be at least 6.4 metres (21 feet) wide and made from stone or gravel.

From then on Ireland's main roads greatly improved and were often better than roads in England.

Superstitions

Lucky trees

Did you know that the luckiest tree was the *caorthann*? That's the **rowan** tree sometimes called the mountain ash. People thought the *caorthann* kept the fairies away. Sometimes a branch was kept in the cow-shed, to be sure of good flows of milk from the cows, or in the house, to prevent fires. Often people didn't like to cut down trees and many trees grew to be huge.

Berries from the rowan or mountain ash. The wood was used to make long-bows.

The remains of an Iron Age roadway at Corlea, County Longford. Made of massive oak trunks, the road was excavated out of the bog in 1985 and you can visit where people travelled over 2,000 years ago. Some people believe the road linked ancient pagan sites.

Lucky numbers

What's your lucky number? 4, 9, 8, 12?

If you lived in Ireland long ago you would probably answer '7'.

The number 7 was special. It was thought that visions about fairies happened every 7 years or that children showed their natural abilities at age 7. Mind you, a curse on a family was said to last for 7 generations (that's hundreds of years!).

There was also another old superstition that if you dreamed the same dream 3 times it was true.

Wide Streets & Hovels

Our Story of Ireland has only three hundred years to go.

Dirt, hovels and booleys

If you lived in Dublin at the start of the eighteenth century, your little house would still be packed close to other houses in narrow, winding streets, which were very crowded, dirty and unhealthy. Life was little better in the countryside, where people lived in crowded hovels.

As a farming child you might be up in the hills with your family's cows. The cows were brought up to graze on the grass in summer. You stayed up there in your 'booley', a small cabin made of stone walls and thatched roof.

Famine and disease were never far away. In the year 1741, you probably had an awful family disaster. This was called *'bliadhain an air'* meaning **'year of the slaughter'**, when about 300,000 people died from starvation in a terrible potato famine. One writer described it as:

... want and misery in every face ... the roads spread with dead and dying bodies; mankind the colour of the docks and nettles which they fed on.

Life was very different for rich people, especially rich Protestants, who were part of the 'ruling class' living in grand big houses in fine grounds.

One of Dublin's famous Georgian doorways, Merrion Square.

Wide streets and bigger cows

Then, at the end of this century, a lot changed. In Dublin narrow, disease-ridden streets and little houses were swept away. Straight wide streets and grand squares were begun in the reign of King George II, so they are called 'Georgian'. Sackville Street (now O'Connell Street), Merrion, Fitzwilliam and Mountjoy Squares as well as fine new buildings such as the Custom House and Four Courts along the Liffey were all built at this time.

In the country, better farming methods meant that farm animals got bigger and healthier. Cows produced more milk. More crops grew. Instead of exhausting the land as before, big landowners learnt to **rotate** the crops from field to field, always leaving some land free to recover. Many of these ideas came from a new society of farmers and country gentlemen called the Royal Dublin Society (RDS).

Fighting to the death!

People might also be up to something quite different in the countryside: **cock fighting**! Roaring their 'team' on. Betting lots of money. Two cocks fought each other in special cockpits, biting and kicking, often with sharp metal spurs fitted to their feet, until one died and the other won. There were even county teams. This cruel sport was made illegal a long time later (in 1835).

Ulster and the linen triangle

Ulster became the wealthiest part of Ireland with the most people, especially the area of Dungannon-Armagh-Belfast called **The Linen Triangle**. Linen-making became very important. Lots of people worked in linen mills or grew flax on farms to make the linen, or got paid to do the spinning at home. Do you know how much linen was exported from Ireland in 1796? If you spread the linen all out it would cover 26,700 miles (or over 42,000 kilometres).

By then, Ireland's population was growing fast. In fact, it had more than doubled, to $4^{1/2}$ million people.

As you can see, the second half of this century was a much better time to live in Ireland. But some people wanted more. They were hatching rebellion!

Rebellion

Nowadays in Ireland you have a chance to run the country or to vote for those who run the country, once you are 18 years old or older. Children have rights too!

Then, in England and Ireland, only wealthy or 'important' Protestants (men only!) were in the Parliament and the Government. Ireland was still controlled by the English king and by English laws.

Quite suddenly new ideas began to come in, from America and France, where people were fighting to get rights for all. They were saying all people are born **equal**. Many leaders even thought these ideas were dangerous and they fought hard to stop people getting equal rights.

So, from about the year 1775 there was a lot of argument and fighting among leaders and people in many countries. During this time Ireland had new freedom and its own new Parliament, at College Green in Dublin. This was for Protestants only. Others wanted more freedom. So in Belfast some Protestant leaders formed the Society of the United Irishmen, looking for rights for all, including Catholics.

In the end an armed **rebellion** was planned for 1798. One leader of the United Irishmen, Theobald **Wolfe Tone**, went to France to get help. French ships and soldiers did arrive, off Bantry, Sligo and Donegal. At one point they took over much of Sligo and Mayo.

English soldiers fought back hard and, anyway, only certain parts of the country joined in the rebellion: places like Antrim, Down, Meath, Wicklow and Wexford. Many Catholic leaders were against it.

The rebellion failed. Thirty thousand people died. The new Irish parliament was abolished by a law called the **Act of Union**: meaning Ireland and Britain were ruled together as one Union by the parliament in London. This caused a lot of division and trouble in Ireland over the next hundred years or so.

Theobald Wolfe Tone – a name to remember

Why? Because he is known as the 'father of Irish republicanism'. He had a dream that Ireland should be a separate country. He helped lead the fight for Irish independence in 1798. How? By bringing an armed force from France to help, but his rebellion failed. What else? He committed suicide in jail, aged 35, while sentenced to death.

And more? He was born in Dublin. A Protestant. A lawyer. Educated at Trinity College Dublin. Is buried at Bodenstown, County Kildare.

1798 action, places and people

County Wexford had a big rebellion and a story all its own. There, 200 Protestant prisoners were burnt to death in a barn at **Scullabogue**. The Wexford rebels were finally defeated at the famous **Battle of Vinegar Hill** near Enniscorthy on 21 June 1798 by British Army General **Gerard Lake** with 10,000 soldiers. General Lake 'took no prisoners', meaning he ordered captured men to be shot dead. When the overall rebellion ended 1,500 people were either executed, deported from the country or flogged.

Then there was **James Napper Tandy**, a leader of the United Irishmen in Dublin. He went to France to organise help but had disagreements with Theobald Wolfe Tone there. However, on 16 September 1798 Napper Tandy arrived at **Rutland Island**, off Donegal, with French weapons but left when things weren't going well. Later he was captured in Hamburg in Germany, brought back to Ireland, sentenced to death, and sent back to France where he died in 1803.

In 1798 Catholics and Protestants fought together for independence. In May they won The Battle of Three Rocks and took control of Wexford town. But in the end the rebellion failed.

Something else happened in 1803

That year a 25-year-old Dublin Protestant called **Robert Emmet** planned another rebellion along with leaders from 1798. He got help from France and secretly stored weapons in Patrick Street near St Patrick's Cathedral in Dublin. But things went wrong. There was an explosion at his arms dump on 16 July, so he started his rebellion early. But it failed when only about 300 men took over Thomas Street and James's Street for two hours. Robert Emmet fled and was captured in the Wicklow Mountains. He made a famous 'speech from the dock' during his court trial and was executed on 20 September 1803.

GUN PO

Smoking Trains

As the new century moved on from 1800, things were looking up for many ordinary people. Yes, Ireland had lost its Parliament and too many people lived on small rented farms. But more people had jobs. Medicine had improved and fewer babies died of disease. The population 'exploded'. By 1841 Ireland had more than 8 million people. And there's more. Great excitement was in the air over brand new travelling machines called steam trains.

No. 186, a Great Southern and Western Railway train, was built in 1879 and is still on the tracks today. It was used (painted different colours) in the film The Great Train Robbery.

Ireland's first train

17 December 1834 was the big day. A huge metal, coal-burning, smoke-belching engine pulled wooden carriages with passengers along metal tracks from Dublin to Kingstown (now Dún Laoghaire).

Mania

Next, steam trains puffed between Belfast, Lisburn and Portadown, carrying people and goods around the Linen Triangle. Soon there was **railway mania**. Every town wanted one. Between 1849 and 1855 railway lines went from Dublin to Cork, to Galway and to Belfast. Within a few years Ireland had 1,127 kilometres (700 miles) of railway. It saved so much time. For instance, Dublin to Belfast by stage-coach took 10 hours. By steam train it took 5$^{1/2}$ hours!

Whoooossshhing the cattle

You are in a field with your mother and father, six sisters and four brothers. It's St John's Eve 1841, Midsummer night. Stars and half moon are shining. Your father lights two bonfires in the field, leaving a wide gap between the two, as he does every year, and you all gather around in great excitement. You sing old songs and dance. Even the three cattle seem to enjoy it. Your landlord, James Synnott, waves as he passes the stone wall in his fine coach and horses. Two cottiers (labourers) who had helped you dig up potatoes on your small farm in County Galway join the gang. Your father whoooossshhes the cattle between the two fires, to protect them from disease and to get rid of tics and other parasites. It's an old Irish belief. A bunch of you follow, yelling and whoooossshhing too. When the fires die down, you help scatter the embers on the field, believing this will bring better growth than last year.

8,000,000
1841
Ireland – population

Death comes Calling

The year is 1845. Suddenly, death strikes all over the country.

A disease made the main food, potatoes, rot in the ground. This disease had a proper name, *phytophthora infestans*. Irish people knew it simply as 'potato blight'. This tragedy is called the Great Famine because more people died than in earlier famines, such as the awful famine of 1741 when 300,000 people died.

This time about 1 million people died.

Imagine the news

Imagine they had television in those days. '*Here is a report from Michael Kennedy in Kilrush, County Clare.*'

I'm standing outside Kilrush workhouse. I see haggard men banging on the door trying to get in. I see mothers crying as their children lie, dying. These helpless creatures are not only unhoused, but often driven off the land. As soon as one horde of houseless and all but naked paupers are dead their numbers double. They in turn pass through the same ordeal of wandering from house to house, or burrowing in bogs or behind ditches, til broken down by privation and exposure to the elements, they seek the workhouse, or die by the roadside.

(This story is from a true report in Kilrush at the time).

A victim of the famine is being taken from his house for burial in Skibbereen, County Cork.

Why did they die?

You might wonder why a potato blight would kill so many people. Ireland's population had 'exploded' and was now over 8 million. About 3 million people relied on potatoes to eat and sell to earn their rent. When something went wrong with the potato crop, these people became hungry and desperate; they left their homes searching for food, began eating grass and nettles, fell sick and died.

People in the west of Ireland suffered the most because far too many families lived on tiny farms, which they rented from a landlord. Often the landlord made the families leave because now they could not pay the rent. This was called 'eviction'.

There were, of course, a lot of kind people who tried to help, including landlords who took pity on the families and let them stay even when they couldn't pay rent. Some people, like a religious group called the Society of Friends, set up soup kitchens and gave out soup, clothes and money.

Eviction: when the potato crop failed and small farmers could not pay their rent, the landlords came with soldiers and battering rams to throw people out of their homes.

Margaret Conway (a model figure) was only 15 when she sailed to America on the Jeanie Johnston with her 12-year-old brother, John. There is no record of her parents on board.

The Workhouse

When people got really desperate, they headed for the big stone workhouse. The workhouses were tough places. People often had to work at breaking stones to get food, usually porridge, potatoes and milk. And families were split up inside. The mother, father and their children had to sleep in different wards. Soon even the workhouses were packed full and many thousands died outside, unable to get in.

Food at last

At first, the Government in London thought the landlords should pay for extra food. But things kept getting worse. At last, from February 1847 the government paid for 'soup kitchens', which gave out 3 million meals a day. This was a great help. It saved thousands of people from dying. But in September that year these kitchens were stopped, because the government insisted that starving people must again go to the workhouses.

Many families died in their own homes, often from fever and disease which could easily spread to others. This meant that many neighbours were afraid to go near the house to bury the family. Instead they knocked down the house with the dead father, mother and children inside. Their house became their grave.

In the 1840s, many people lived in simple cottages such as these and all the family worked hard to grow their own food. When the potato crop failed there was no way to feed the family.

BARF

A disease called cholera

Imagine you lived through all this. Horrible. Five years it lasted, this Great Famine. All around you, hungry and dying people. Your best friend Magdelene, dead. Your favourite uncle, Daniel, dead. Then more. You get really sick in your stomach and start vomiting terribly. It's that new disease called **cholera**. You survive, but much later you hear that cholera was caused by infections from dirty water in towns like yours, Clonmel. You hear that 35,000 Irish people died from cholera in those years.

Emigration and 'coffin ships'

The Great Famine started a trend in emigration as hundreds of thousands of people left Ireland to try for new lives. Most sailed from Cobh in County Cork for America and some went to Britain, Canada and Australia. Thousands died of hunger and disease, packed in like cattle, on the '**coffin ships**' during the six-week boat journey to America.

This terrible experience was to have a lasting effect on those who survived. A deep anti-British feeling lay in the hearts of many emigrants, especially in America, and was passed on down through the generations.

The Famine ship, the Jeanie Johnston, made 16 voyages from Ireland to America and Canada between 1848 and 1855.

The bleak and shocking years of the Great Famine left scars on Ireland for a very long time. The population, for one, was much smaller and continued to drop for a hundred years and more. But right now, it's time for a walk. Time to look up. Time for tall monuments and 'monster meetings'!

6,500,000

GREAT FAMINE

Ireland—population

Statues with a Story

As we move past the middle of the 1800s some strong leaders try to bring
about big changes in Ireland. If only we could listen to what their statues tell us!
Why don't we give it a try? After all, if we look around us we see that history is everywhere.
For instance, what do you know about the place where you live? The name of your street? Or village? Or town?
Their names tell you their own story, something about what happened in the past.

Strolling down O'Connell Street

If we take a stroll down O'Connell Street in the centre of the capital city of Ireland, Dublin, we will find out more
about Ireland's story. We start on O'Connell Bridge, over the River Liffey, looking down O'Connell Street.

Daniel O'Connell and his 'monster meetings'!

Do you know why the names are O'Connell Bridge and
O'Connell Street? They are called after Daniel O'Connell,
from Kerry.

We cross into O'Connell Street itself and see a statue of a
man, standing up high. Known as 'The Liberator', Daniel
O'Connell was a great leader and a wonderful speaker, who
did a lot to make sure that Roman Catholics got a fair deal.
He lived from 1775 to 1847. Daniel O'Connell spoke at
huge open-air rallies called 'monster meetings'. During
one year 120,000 people turned out to hear him at
Limerick, 200,000 came to hear him at Charleville in
County Cork, 500,000 at Nenagh in County Tipperary,
another 500,000 at Waterford and when he called a
'monster' meeting for the Hill of Tara in County Meath
900,000 people turned up!

He was trying to show the Government in London that
Irish people wanted their own parliament back in Dublin
but he didn't succeed. Still, he did help

Catholics get other rights, like being a judge or being
elected to Parliament in London. These changes were called
'Catholic Emancipation'.

Daniel O'Connell made a special point of holding
peaceful meetings. O'Connell himself was elected to
Parliament. He also became Lord Mayor of Dublin, even
though he was a Kerryman, from near Caherciveen. He was
very popular. In fact, when
there was a ceremony to
lay the foundation stone
for his statue in
O'Connell Street about
half a million people
turned up!

Statue of Daniel
O'Connell, 'The
Liberator', O'Connell
Street, Dublin.

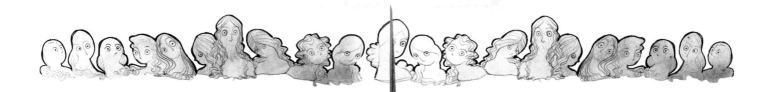

'Big Jim'

If we continue walking up O'Connell Street and look across to the centre of the street, we see another statue: that's **'Big Jim'** Larkin. He came later in Ireland's story. Big Jim was all for workers' rights, to make sure they got proper pay and proper jobs.

The General Post Office

We pass the **GPO** (General Post Office). There was a lot of fighting and shooting there during the Easter Rising, 1916. You can still see the bullet holes in the pillars.

The Spire

On to the new Spire. Look up, right up! The Spire was put up in 2003. You might even remember it being built.

TO
CHARLES STEWART PARNELL

"NO·MAN·HAS·A·RIGHT·TO·FIX·THE·
BOUNDARY·TO·THE·MARCH·OF·A·NATION·
NO·MAN·HAS·A·RIGHT·
TO·SAY·TO·HIS·COUNTRY·
THUS·FAR·SHALT·THOU·
GO·AND·NO·FURTHER·
WE·HAVE·NEVER·
ATTEMPTED·TO·FIX·
THE·NE·PLUS·ULTRA·
TO·THE·PROGRESS·OF·
IRELANDS·NATIONHOOD·
AND·WE·NEVER·SHALL"

ʒo roinbiʒioʒoia
éine oa clainn

UL-
STER
CON-
NACT
LEIN-
STER
MUN-
STER

The Charles Stewart Parnell
monument at the end of
O'Connell Street, Dublin.

Who's Charles Stewart Parnell?

On we stroll. We're looking for a big, tall, pointy monument at the end of O'Connell Street – the Parnell monument (see left) – named after **Charles Stewart Parnell**, from Avondale in County Wicklow.

Parnell, who lived from 1846 to 1891, was so important at the time that he was even called the 'Uncrowned King of Ireland'. Charles Stewart Parnell played a very big part in the story of Ireland, in two important ways:

1. **LAND.** Remember the Famine? Thousands of starving farmers wandered around helplessly because they couldn't pay the rent. Parnell led a big campaign and got small farmers a better deal. They were to have fairer rents and it was made harder for landlords to evict them. They could also buy their land at a fair price.

2. **HOME RULE.** Remember how Ireland's parliament in Dublin was abolished? Ireland was now ruled from Parliament in London. Charles Stewart Parnell was elected to that Parliament. He led another campaign to get Ireland **Home Rule**: meaning rule from home, in Dublin, though Ireland would still be connected to Great Britain. However, many people disagreed with Home Rule. Most Protestants in Ulster wanted to be ruled from London, not Dublin. Other people called **Fenians** made plans to fight for complete freedom for Ireland. Many in Britain still wanted to control Ireland. As you can imagine this caused a lot of trouble and in the end Parnell failed to get Ireland's Parliament back in Dublin. But he had put Home Rule 'on the map'.

Katherine O'Shea

During the late 1880s Charles Stewart Parnell had a love affair with a married woman, **Katherine ('Kitty') O'Shea**, causing a huge scandal. While Parnell is today remembered as a great Irish leader, this affair ruined his political career. Eventually Charles Stewart married Kitty.

Artramon House, County Wexford is typical of the 'big houses' of this period.

Anna and Frances Parnell – names to remember

Anna and Frances (or Fanny) were sisters of Charles Stewart Parnell. They set up the Ladies' Land League in Ireland and America to continue the struggle for farmers' rights when Charles Stewart was put in Kilmainham Jail in Dublin. Anna was especially strong on women's rights and fell out with Parnell over this.

As you can see, Irish people lived through many changes during the 1800s. You've heard about great famine and great leaders. Our next three chapters tell the story of hedge schools, booming Belfast and new ball games. First, learning to learn.

It's time to pause, look back a little and see what's going on in school.

The right to learn

We take it for granted that we go to school. We have what is called a **right** to education. The law says so. It wasn't always this way in Ireland.

Back when Gaelic chiefs like the O'Neills, O'Briens and O'Connors were in charge, most children never even learnt to read or write. But the children of richer or more 'important' families learnt from wonderful poets and scholars in what are sometimes called '**bardic schools**'. A bard or a *file* taught poetry or history or Brehon law or medicine in the Gaelic language or Latin.

What about ordinary children?

Much later, during the 1700s when Catholic schools were forbidden, ordinary children began learning in the **hedge schools**. In time, children could quite openly go to school in some hall or house. Teachers moved around from place to place teaching, normally in English. These schools continued into the 1800s.

Many children couldn't afford to buy books. In 1810, a farmworker earned about 2 or 3 shillings (about 20 to 30 cents) a week.

But a spelling book cost about $1^{1/2}$ shillings (16 cents) and a geography book as much as 6 shillings (about 60 cents), about two weeks' wages!

So, many children learnt **by rote**, that is by learning their lessons off by heart, copying the teacher.

Boys from de la Salle school, 1902.

☞ Girls learning to weave and spin in a convent school in Cobh (then Queenstown), County Cork in the late 1800s.

Turf for the master

Often parents were too poor to pay the teacher and so their children had no schooling. Many children walked the country lanes to school in their **bare feet**, maybe even carrying bundles of turf or eggs from the farm to pay the teacher. At school they called the teacher **'master'** and the master was a very important person. **Slapping** or hitting the children with a cane, or stick, was allowed!

In the end as many as 400,000 children were taught in all kinds of schools and sometimes with very strange books.

That's why the Government decided to bring in a single system for the whole country from the year 1831. This was the start of the National Schools, which still exist today. The idea was that all children would get a good education with properly trained teachers and proper text-books.

It was hoped that children of all religions would be taught together, but soon the Churches insisted on having their own separate schools.

By the year 1900 most Irish children could read, write, spell and count.

A City is Born

Looking north now, we'll find out what's happening in Belfast.

Booming Belfast

For most of our story Belfast was a very small town, with less than 1,000 people. Dublin was Ireland's main city. Then Belfast grew, fast. In the years from 1841 to 1901 the number of people living in Belfast rose from 70,000 to 349,180. Belfast was becoming very important.

There was also a lot of trouble in Belfast. Often there were terrible riots in the streets between Protestants and Catholics. Most of the people were Protestant and very proud of being British. As time went by more and more Catholics wanted Irish Home Rule.

City of industry

Now we know that Belfast has an interesting story to tell. The city grew and grew because all kinds of important factories and industries were built there, employing thousands of people. Belfast's industries were famous around the world.

Big factories made **linen, clothing, ropes** for ships, **whiskey, cigarettes** and machines of all sorts. **Shipbuilding** was especially important. Some of the world's biggest ships were built in Belfast shipyards owned by a company called Harland and Wolff. That's where the *Titanic* ship was built.

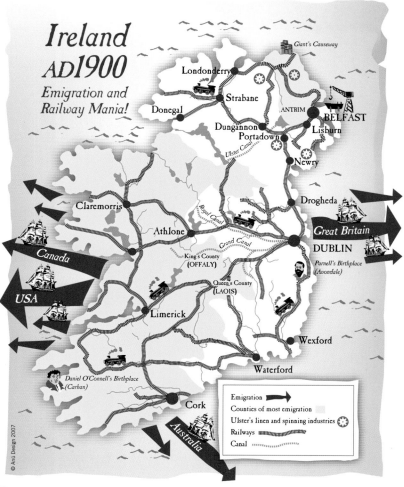

Ireland AD1900
Emigration and Railway Mania!

Giant's Causeway
Londonderry
Strabane
Donegal
ANTRIM
BELFAST
Dungannon
Portadown
Lisburn
Ulster Canal
Newry
Claremorris
Drogheda
Athlone
Royal Canal
Great Britain
Canada
Grand Canal
DUBLIN
King's County (OFFALY)
Parnell's Birthplace (Avondale)
USA
Queen's County (LAOIS)
Limerick
Wexford
Waterford
Daniel O'Connell's Birthplace (Carhan)
Australia
Cork

© Anú Design 2007

Emigration
Counties of most emigration
Ulster's linen and spinning industries
Railways
Canal

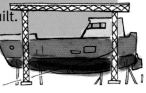

The last photograph of the Titanic taken by Fr Browne, as the ship left Cobh (Queenstown).

The Titanic

When the *Titanic* was launched it was the biggest ship in the world. It was more than 245 metres (800 feet) long and said to be unsinkable. But at 11.40pm on 14 April 1912, on her first voyage across the Atlantic Ocean, the *Titanic* struck a huge ice-berg which cut a 92-metre (300 foot) hole in the hull. The 'unsinkable' ship began to sink. Panic! Not enough lifeboats! Out of 2,201 passengers and crew 1,490 drowned in the freezing waters. The *Belfast Newsletter* newspaper reported it as 'the most appalling shipping disaster in the history of the world.'

Our story has entered its final hundred years, into a century of great change, from motor cars and television to flying to the Moon. Fantastic! But what was going on in Miss Hayes's Hotel in Thurles? That's next.

The Hound of Culainn

Do you know how Gaelic games started ? When hurling began?
Who the Hound of Culainn was?

How about a game of hurling?

1872: Saturday afternoon, 15 November. King's County (Offaly) v Queen's County (Laois). No written rules. No fighting. 21 players on each side. Hurling was going through its 'golden age', becoming very popular, and was played a little differently from place to place. Landlords organised games.

1884: Saturday 1 November. A meeting is being held in the billiard-room of Miss Hayes's Commercial Hotel in Thurles, County Tipperary. A group of men are trying to start up a new organisation for Gaelic games. Hurling, for one, was not being played much outside Dublin due to so many people leaving the land after the Famine. One of the organisers is Michael Cusack, a teacher who was very fond of rugby, cricket and athletics.

In fact, athletics is what those at the meeting mostly talk about: running races, the high jump, long jump, throwing the hammer, slinging the 56lbs, throwing the 16lbs and so on. These are the sort of games which went all the way back, before Christianity, to the Tailteann games of old,

which were held at Teltown in County Meath for the first week in August.

Those at Miss Hayes's hotel did start a new athletics group. They called it 'The Gaelic Association for the Preservation and Cultivation of our National Pastimes'. Within a few weeks this mouthful was shortened to **The Gaelic Athletic Association.**

The Gaelic Athletic Association was part of a push for things Irish, like the Irish language and especially the idea of an independent Ireland.

As we saw, the GAA drew ideas from ancient Irish sports such as the old **Tailteann** games. These games were traced back more than 2,500 years, to sporting competitions held at Tara in 632BC by the High King 'Lugh-of-the-long-arm'. Much later they became contests between the northern and southern Uí Neill clans to decide who would be King of Tara (High King). Often the games became very violent as the rival clans clashed.

Gaelic football

For at least two hundred years before the GAA began children (and adults) played a game where you kicked a ball and carried it in your hands. There were all sorts of different rules and even different shaped balls. Soon the GAA had one set of rules for everyone: 15 players a side, playing the new game of **Gaelic football**.

Gaelic football took off in a big way. Thousands of people began turning up for games. The GAA was planning ahead. In the year 1913 they bought some land at St Jones's Road on Dublin's northside. Much later they built a headquarters and national stadium there, calling it **Croke Park** after the Roman Catholic Archbishop of Cashel, Thomas W. Croke. Archbishop Croke supported the GAA from that very first meeting at Miss Hayes's Commercial Hotel in Thurles.

Kerry and Tyrone in action in Croke Park, 2003.

The legendary Cork hurler, Christy Ring (1920–1979), in action.

Hurling, camogie and handball

Hurling was also given firm rules: **15-a-side** and played with a **hurley stick** (*camán*) and *sliotar* (leather ball). **Camogie**, for women and girls, was similar to hurling. **Handball** was another GAA sport. Generally Gaelic games were played by Catholics. Many Protestants, especially in Ulster, did not want to become part of this new push for things Gaelic or for the idea of an independent Ireland.

People were encouraged to use the Irish language when they talked about Gaelic games:

Football was *peil*

Hurling was *iománaíocht*

Camogie was *camógaíocht*

Handball was *liathróid láimhe*

An early hurley stick (or camán).

What's in a name?

What about the word **'Gaelic'** itself? Where does it come from?

Well, it seems, we have to go back at least twelve hundred years when 'Gael' meant the native people of Ireland. But if we go back even further the experts think 'Gael' may come from 'gwyddel'. Gwyddel? Yes, from Wales. And, in Welsh 'gwydd' means 'wild' or 'savage'.

CúChulainn, the hound of Culainn

Legends show us how old hurling is. The most famous legend is about CúChulainn who was said to exist in the mist of old Celtic times. This is the story:

CúChulainn's proper name was Setanta, nephew of Conor MacNessa, King of Ulster. King Conor ruled from Ulster's capital, *Emain Macha*, a name taken from the goddess Macha and from which *Armagh* might have got its name. Setanta won fear and fame by fighting to victory over a band of Boys' Troop who were the sons of the great Red Branch fighters of Ulster.

One day Setanta was playing hurling with the Boys' Troop when King Conor rode by. The King asked Setanta to come with him to a feast at the castle of his friend Culainn. Setanta said he would go later, after the hurling game was finished. This he did. But Setanta hadn't arrived at the feast by the time darkness fell. Inside, Culainn asked King Conor if anyone else was due to arrive. Conor said 'no', forgetting about Setanta. Culainn then bolted his door and let loose his mighty hound to roam around, guarding the place.

Soon, Setanta arrived, still carrying his red bronze *camán* (hurley stick) and silver *sliotar* (ball). The hound attacked Setanta, who had no weapons but the stick and sliotar. Setanta hurled a fierce shot and the sliotar stuck in the throat of the hound. Setanta then grabbed the hound by the hind legs, swung him and crashed him against a rock, killing him. When Culainn and the others came out and saw this, Culainn went into great grief over his faithful hound. But Setanta made a solemn promise. He himself would guard Culainn's house until he could get him another great hound. From that night on Setanta was granted the name of **CúChulainn**, Hound of Culainn.

On to workers' rights, women's rights and secret plans.

Fighting for a Cause

Our great journey is now moving through the twentieth century, a century of amazing changes. People will drive cars without a horse! They will speak to brothers and sisters thousands of miles away, without going there. Turn on a switch and there will be light. And, sadly, there will be a lot of fighting. Ireland will be divided.

'Big Jim' Larkin

It was Sunday 31 August 1913. A lot of children were very hungry still. But that did not stop them and their parents coming along in their thousands to Sackville Street (now O'Connell Street), Dublin. Suddenly up on the balcony of the Imperial Hotel he appeared. Jim Larkin.

'Big Jim' Larkin.

'Big Jim' Larkin calling for workers' rights.

'Workers … of Dublin … !' Not much more was heard of Big Jim's booming voice as he was hauled off by two policemen.

After Big Jim's arrest masses of police batoned the crowd. Two people died. Hundreds were injured, including policemen.

Jim Larkin was fighting for a cause: the cause of **workers' rights**. About 100,000 Dublin people lived in awful, dirty, unhealthy flats called tenements. Jim Larkin had helped organise workers in a new trade union, the **Irish Transport And General Workers' Union (ITGWU)**. 'Big Jim' called workers out on strike, many strikes, for proper pay, proper hours of work for tram workers, farm workers, railwaymen, dockers and many more. Strikes meant the workers refused to work and so had no pay and soon no food. Soup kitchens were set up to try and feed the starving workers and their families. Employers hit back, banding together, locking out those workers who joined the union.

English workers sent shiploads of food for those locked out.

As many as 25,000 workers were locked out from September 1913 to January 1914. By then food ran out. Help from England stopped.

James Connolly and the Irish Citizen Army

Jim Larkin was put in prison in October 1913. **James Connolly** took over. He formed the **Irish Citizen Army**. Workers were trained to fight with guns. This became important later.

In the end, the hungry and desperate strikers were forced to go back to work, provided they left the trade union. They had been defeated by the employers.

WE SERVE NEITHER KING NOR KAISER, BUT IRELAND!

HEAD OFFICE. IRISH TRANSPORT AND GENERAL WORKERS' UNION

Irish Citizen Army parading outside Liberty Hall, Dublin.

We want to vote!

Ireland was still ruled from London. In Britain **Emmeline Pankhurst** began a union in 1903 demanding votes for women. Soon, a women's league in Ireland did the same. In England **Emily Davison** was killed protesting for the vote when she threw herself under the King's horse during the 1913 Derby. Finally, in 1918 British and Irish women were allowed to vote and run for parliament … but only those over 30 years old. It was a long time before laws were passed giving women equal opportunities in jobs and pay. About another 50 years!

VOTES!

WE WANT VOTES

VOTES FOR WOMEN

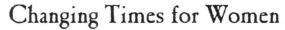

Just imagine

Imagine you are 12 years old in the year 1900. You are dreaming of what you would like to be when you grow up: own your own farm, be a famous athlete, a teacher, doctor, or get a good job in the biscuit factory, like a manager. How about maybe even getting elected to the Parliament and making people's lives better? Problem is, you're a **girl**. And women are not allowed to do most of those things. The law says so. Most things were run by men. They even got paid more than women. A married woman, for instance, couldn't own land or property in her own name.

Right across the world women were beginning to 'fight' for their own cause.

Changing Times for Women

❀ Women were allowed into the 1900 Olympic Games.

❀ China banned female foot-binding in 1911.
(In this custom girls had their smaller toes bandaged underneath their feet, to make their feet small and dainty; but it was painful and crippling).

❀ New Zealand was the only country where women could vote in national elections.

War & Rebellion: Ireland is torn in two

These were times of secret plans and secret plots. War and rebellion were in the air.

In Europe after 1914 a war had spread far and wide to become the **First World War**, with Britain on one side and Germany on the other. While that was going on, secret plans were hatched at home to smuggle in shipments of arms. People were plotting to fight for very different things, leading to rebellion in Ulster and insurrection in Dublin.

In the four years between 1912 and 1916 Ireland's people were torn between two different futures, either:

❀ Keep the Union with Great Britain and continue to be ruled from London or
❀ Get Home Rule for Ireland and have a Parliament in Dublin.

A Howth Mauser gun used by the rebels, Easter 1916. Smugglers brought the gun into Howth, County Dublin, from Germany.

'Ulster will fight'

The Government in London decided to give Home Rule to Ireland. Many Protestants, especially in Ulster, plotted to stop it. They were called **Unionists** because they wanted to keep the Union with Britain. Their leader was **Edward Carson** (see opposite). Unionists said rule from Dublin would mean rule by the Roman Catholic Church. Also, Belfast and east Ulster were doing very well from big industries like shipbuilding and linen. Unionists didn't want things to change.

Unionists formed an army called the **Ulster Volunteer Force** of about 90,000 men. Secretly, they smuggled in 25,000 rifles on the *Clyde Valley* and *Fanny* ships.

Unionists had a saying: *Ulster will Fight and Ulster will be Right*.

There was another saying: *Ireland unfree shall never be at Peace*.

This was said by **Pádraig Pearse**. He was a leader who wanted **Home Rule** for Ireland. Later, he changed his mind and helped in a secret plan to fight for complete freedom from Britain.

Home Rule would mean a Parliament in Dublin to make laws for Ireland. But Ireland would still be connected to Britain and the king. Most Irish people, including most Catholics, were happy with that. Their leader was **John Redmond**.

John Redmond said Irish men should fight with Britain in the First World War against Germany and many did.

After the Easter Rising, 1916, the corner of Sackville Street (now O'Connell Street) and Eden Quay lay in ruins.

The secret plan

Pádraig Pearse and his comrades planned an armed insurrection against Britain. They had a fighting force called the **Irish Volunteers**, and guns smuggled into Howth, County Dublin, aboard the *Asgard* yacht. Some leaders secretly formed a Military Council of the Irish Republican Brotherhood. James Connolly's **Irish Citizen Army** joined in. They planned more guns from Germany, enough for a countrywide Rising on **Easter Sunday 1916.**

The *Aud* ship, carrying 20,000 guns, arrived off the Kerry coast. But it wasn't met due to a mix-up and the German captain sank it, to avoid being captured.

The Rising went ahead anyway, but mostly only in Dublin, on Easter Monday

Pádraig Pearse.

1916. They captured the General Post Office (GPO) in Sackville Street (now O'Connell Street) and a number of other places. But after six days of heavy bombardment by the British Army, the leaders surrendered.

About 230 ordinary Dublin people and about 200 fighters were killed. Much of the city was in rubble.

The Rising was not very popular with the people. But when the British Army executed the leaders more and more Irish people turned in support of the Rising and in favour of a complete break from Great Britain. One of the leaders **Eamon de Valera,** was not executed, because he had been born in America and therefore he was an American citizen. He became very important later.

Constance Markievicz

This rather grand-speaking woman with a Polish husband and a Sligo mother ran soup kitchens for workers and fought in the 1916 Rising. She was the first-ever woman elected to Parliament, in 1918, for Sinn Féin. When she died in 1927 many working-class people lined the streets for her funeral.

☞ Constance Markievicz was Second-in-Command in St Stephen's Green during the 1916 Rising.

The story of Ireland is now moving on fast. The island we know today is taking shape. In the north and in the south people are fighting and struggling for very different futures. Ireland is becoming divided into two parts.

Ireland is Divided

Let's catch up on all the fighting.

The island splits, North and South

Remember the Ulster Volunteer Force preparing to fight? They wanted rule from London not Dublin. Remember also the **Rising** in Dublin at Easter 1916? They wanted an all-Ireland independent republic completely free from Britain. In the end, neither side got what they really wanted when Ireland was divided into two parts, north and south.

The big changes happened in the years 1919 to 1923. Before that period Ireland was one complete country of 32 counties ruled from London. After it, Ireland was divided for the first time. A new place called **Northern Ireland** was set up with a new parliament in Belfast. Northern Ireland consisted of 6 counties: Down, Antrim, Armagh, Londonderry (also called Derry), Tyrone and Fermanagh.

The other 26 counties formed a new country called the **Irish Free State** with a new parliament in Dublin. Some fought on for the all-Ireland republic.

Hearing different signals

North and South had different radio stations too.

On 1 January 1926 the Dublin Broadcasting Station started, joined by another in Cork the following year. These were called 2RN (a name taken from the ending of the Irish song, 'come back to Erin'.) Much later 2RN became **Radio Éireann** and then **RTÉ** (*Radio Telefís Éireann*). Northern Ireland's radio station was the BBC (British Broadcasting Corporation), which started broadcasting, mostly around Belfast, in 1924.

Changing world

❋ 1901: First transatlantic radio signal sent from England and instant coffee is invented.

❋ 1903: Orville and Wilbur Wright fly 260 metres (853 feet) in a flying machine on Kitty Hawk beach, North Carolina, USA.

❋ 1908: Model T Ford cars are manufactured, USA. Cars are becoming more affordable as they start to be mass produced.

❋ 1922: Canadian doctor first uses insulin to help people with diabetes.

One of the first makes of car in Ireland.

Countdown to a changing Ireland

JANUARY 1919: An 'illegal' Dáil Éireann (parliament) is set up in Dublin by those who want an all-Ireland republic. Eamon de Valera is its President. At the same time a **War of Independence** is started by those wanting to fight Great Britain for that republic.

DECEMBER 1920: '**Northern Ireland**' is set up in six counties of Ulster.

JULY 1921: The War of Independence ends, making way for negotiations in London between the British Government and Irish leaders.

DECEMBER 1921: The negotiators in London agree a **Treaty**, to set up a new country in 26 counties called the '**Irish Free State**'.

JANUARY 1922: In Dublin members of Dáil Éireann vote to accept the Treaty by 64 votes to 57. Opponents of the Treaty leave the Dáil to fight on for more independence.

APRIL 1922: A bitter **Civil War** starts between those who support the Treaty and those who oppose it. **Michael Collins** was for the Treaty and **Eamon de Valera** was against it.

AUGUST 1922: Michael Collins is ambushed and shot dead. For many Michael Collins was the most exciting and charismatic leader of the pro-Treaty forces. Overall, 2,000 die during the Civil War.

MAY 1923: The Civil War ends in a victory for those for the Treaty. This means the Irish Free State (26 counties) and Northern Ireland (6 counties) stay in existence and Ireland stays divided.

British soldiers arresting civilians outside the Custom House, during the War of Independence.

Armoured car from the Civil War.

Collins, Carson and de Valera – Comrades and Enemies

Three leaders from these stirring times: **Michael Collins** (left), born Clonakilty, County Cork, a strong military leader of great promise who split with his comrade **Eamon de Valera** (right) over the Treaty, killed aged 32. **Edward Carson**, Ulster Unionist leader born in Dublin, powerful speaker, opposed Collins and de Valera, helped set up Northern Ireland, lived on as British Government minister and lawyer, died aged 81. **Eamon de Valera**, born in New York, made the biggest mark on Ireland, led a new political party, Fianna Fáil, became Taoiseach for many years and President for 14 years, died aged 93, the oldest of the three.

Waiting for a train

While a lot was happening elsewhere, all the political conflict, arms shipments, warfare and so on, ordinary life went on. Like waiting for a train. The year 1922 was the high point for Irish railways. Ireland had almost 5,600 kilometres (3,454 miles) of track. Most of this was standard gauge track which means 1 metre 60 (5 feet 3 inches) wide. The rest, and this includes the famous West Clare track, was narrow gauge or almost 1 metre (3 feet) wide. So Ireland needed two different types of train! Not surprisingly, one type had to go and that was the narrow gauge. It took until 1961 for all the narrow gauge railway lines and trains to be removed.

'Maedb' was one of Ireland's largest steam locomotives, built in 1939 in Dublin.

Going different ways

Even the railways were divided in the new Ireland. The 26-county Irish Free State had the Great Southern Railway company, while the Great Northern Railway ran things in 6-county Northern Ireland.

☞ A butter churn swirled the milk around and around to make butter.

Farming in the 1920s and 1930s

Farming at this time was done mostly by **hand** and hard physical work. Farmers did not have the **technology** and **machines** they have today. Cows were hand-milked. Milk went sour very quickly so it had to be delivered to houses twice a day, by horse-drawn carts. When pasteurisation came, after 1924, the milk lasted longer. In the countryside, farmers' wives 'churned' the milk to make butter. The men walked their cattle to the town or village to sell them in street fairs. Generally farmers got poor prices and, much later, they had milk strikes and protests to get a better deal.

Sitting in different buildings

More and more the two governments went their separate ways. In Dublin the new Irish parliament moved into a fine old building called **Leinster House** (see picture) in Kildare Street, built almost 200 years earlier for the Earl of Kildare. In the North, Ulster Unionists were determined to show their separation from Dublin. As a mark of that separation Northern Ireland got a very grand parliament specially built at **Stormont** outside Belfast in 1932.

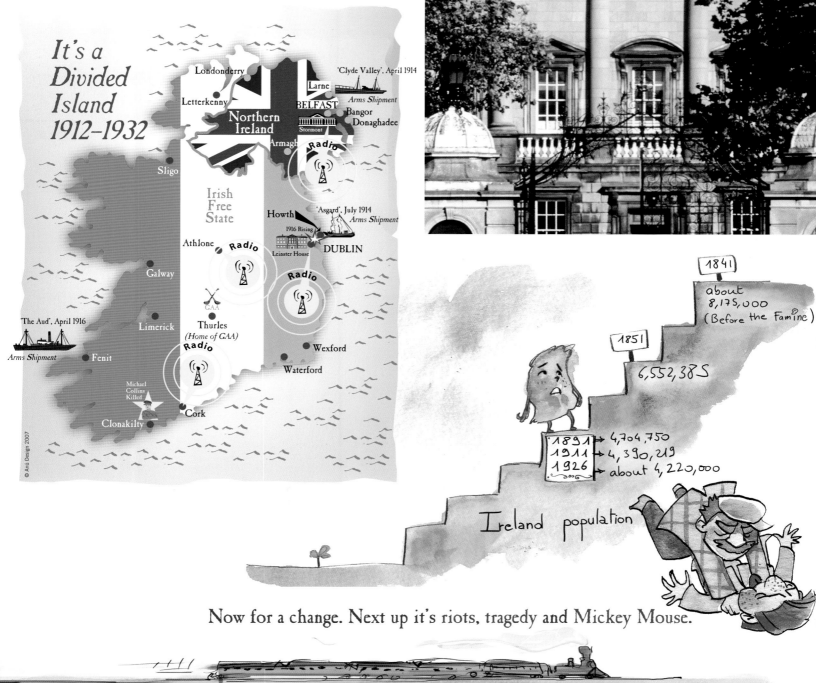

It's a
Divided
Island
1912–1932

Londonderry
Letterkenny
'Clyde Valley', April 1914
Larne
BELFAST
Northern Ireland
Stormont
Arms Shipment
Bangor
Donaghadee
Armagh
Radio
Sligo
Irish Free State
Athlone
Radio
Howth
'Asgard', July 1914
Arms Shipment
1916 Rising
Leinster House
DUBLIN
Radio
Galway
GAA
Thurles
(Home of GAA)
Limerick
Radio
Wexford
Waterford
'The Aud', April 1916
Arms Shipment
Fenit
Michael Collins Killed
Clonakilty
Cork

© Anú Design 2007

1841 about 8,175,000 (Before the Famine)

1851 6,552,385

1891 → 4,704,750
1911 → 4,390,219
1926 → about 4,220,000

Ireland population

Now for a change. Next up it's riots, tragedy and Mickey Mouse.

Changing Times

In the 1930s things were hotting up in Europe but settling down in Ireland.

'Plane Crazy'

The cinema arrived in Ireland. You laughed your head off at Mickey Mouse in 'Plane Crazy', a cartoon film without sound by a new American film-maker, Walt Disney.

Tragedy

Ireland's first cinema was opened by James Joyce, author of Ulysses. It was called the Volta and opened in Mary Street, Dublin on 20 December 1909. Some cinemas were a bit strange and unsafe: like the shed in Drumcollogher in County Limerick where people had to climb a wooden ladder to get in. On 5 September 1926 a terrible tragedy happened there. During a film a fire broke out at the film projector, caused by a candle touching the reel of film. There was panic as people tried to escape. Forty-eight people died. Cinemas and films were made safer after this. By 1930 Ireland had more than 260 cinemas and film halls.

What a riot!

A theatre in Dublin called the Abbey had its fill of trouble too. Plays about Ireland by great Irish writers like **William Butler Yeats**, **John M. Synge**, **Sean O'Casey** and **George Bernard Shaw** often caused heated debate and even riots! In 1924 the Irish Free State government gave money and support to the Abbey, making it Ireland's 'national' theatre.

At the beginning of the 20th century, TB was a killer disease in Ireland. Here we see children getting Irish Red Cross care in the fresh air of the Dublin mountains at the IRC Preventorium, Ballyroan, Rathfarnham, County Dublin.

Changing Ireland

Things were moving on in Ireland, for better and worse. Very many Irish people, North and South, still died from a disease called **tuberculosis** (TB) which damaged the lungs. But in the late 1930s and 1940s doctors began giving the BCG vaccine to children. New drugs, like streptomycin, came along. TB then stopped being a big killer.

Perhaps the biggest and brightest change for ordinary people was the simple **light switch**. Although electric street lighting existed in the 1880s, electricity came to most ordinary homes after the Electricity

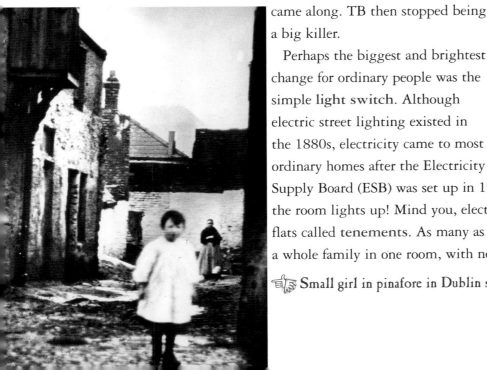

Collecting water was hard work and had to be done every day. Water well, County Cork c.1930s.

Supply Board (ESB) was set up in 1927. Imagine the first time – a simple switch and the room lights up! Mind you, electricity took a long time to reach many city slum flats called **tenements**. As many as 100,000 poor Dubliners lived in tenements, often a whole family in one room, with no running water and a shared outdoor toilet.

Small girl in pinafore in Dublin slums, early 1900s.

Changing world

* 1917: The Russian Revolution is turning Russia into a Communist country. Communism was an idea of 'workers' rights' where farms, factories, government and so on would be run 'by the people for the people' through just one political party, the Communist Party.
* 1928: Penicillin, the first antibiotic, discovered by Alexander Fleming, helps cure many diseases.
* 1930: Uruguay wins the first football World Cup; world population reaches 2 billion.
* 1931: World's tallest building the Empire State Building in New York is finished.
* 1933: Adolf Hitler becomes Chancellor (leader) of Germany.

Flying high

Something amazing began 'taking off'. Travel by **air**! In 1928 Dubliner **Col. James Fitzmaurice** co-piloted the first-ever flight from Europe across the Atlantic, from a bumpy field at Baldonnell, County Dublin … just missing a stray sheep … to a frozen lake off Newfoundland. Later, people were flying between Foynes, County Limerick, and America in seaplanes. These 'flying boats' (see photo) would land at sea outside New York and passengers were brought in by ferry. Foynes was a watery beginning for the future Shannon airport.

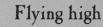

'Gateways' to the world

Flights between Belfast and Renfrew, Scotland, began in 1933. Aer Lingus started in 1936, with a flight to Bristol. **Collinstown** (Dublin) Airport (see photo), which opened in 1940, soon had safety 'blackouts' during the Second World War. Once, the airport's windows were 'blackened' with more than 2,000 metres of material (so bombers couldn't spot any lights)! **Shannon Airport** started in 1947, an important 'gateway' between Europe and America.

A new sort of war

There was still trouble between Britain and the Irish Free State. For instance, under the Treaty Britain still controlled three Irish ports for defence reasons, two in County Cork and one in County Donegal. The Irish side still owed Britain £104 million in land loans. Members of Dáil Éireann still had to take an Oath to the British King. That's why the 'economic war' was started with Britain in 1932 by the new Irish Free State government, led by Eamon de Valera. He refused to pay back the loans and stopped the Oath to the King. Britain hit back and put special duties (taxes) on Ireland's biggest business, cattle and dairy goods, making them hard to sell in Britain. De Valera put duties on certain British goods like coal and machinery coming into Ireland. This 'war' ended in 1938 with an Agreement: De Valera's side would pay back just £10 million of the loans; Britain would give up the three Irish ports and both countries would buy and sell goods more easily.

And there was more – a new name

Yes, the Irish Free State got a new name, Éire, in 1937. That's when the people voted for a new Constitution and more freedom from Britain. Northern Ireland remained tied to Britain under its long-standing Unionist Prime Minister James Craig (called Viscount Craigavon). By then the island's total population had fallen to about 4,248,000.

Ration books and glimmermen

We come now to a very important time in our story; a time in Éire called **The Emergency (1939–1945)**, when gas for cooking was rationed, food was scarce and people used **coupons** from **ration books** to buy butter, tea and bread. It was a time of the **glimmermen,** special inspectors who snooped around and cut off your gas, if you used too much!

Why did all this happen?

It was the Second World War. The years were 1939 to 1945, when about 55 million people died. Terrible fighting was taking place and travel was very dangerous. To bring in vital supplies Éire started its own shipping company **Irish Shipping Limited** with its own ships.

Who was fighting?

Mainly Great Britain, France and America on one side against Germany (led by **Adolf Hitler**), Italy and Japan. Hitler's side lost. Éire took no part and stayed **neutral**. This made Taoiseach **Eamon de Valera** very unpopular with Britain's Prime Minister **Winston Churchill**, who wished Britain still controlled those three ports in Cork and Donegal. Northern Ireland did fight. Its ports and land were used by British and American battleships, warplanes and soldiers. Northern Ireland's farmers and businesses did very well supplying food and all kind of things for the War.

Irish Taoiseach Eamon de Valera and Britain's Prime Minister Winston Churchill fell out over the Second World War.

Adolf Hitler loved to make speeches.

Tragedy in the Belfast Blitz

Twice during 1941 German planes bombed Belfast killing more than 1,000 people and damaging about 56,000 homes. One night that year German bombs hit Dublin's North Strand area, killing 34 people.

While Northern Ireland's sacrifices in the War strengthened its links with Britain, Éire became even more separate by calling itself the **Republic of Ireland** in 1949.

After the Blitz: view of Belfast's Bridge Sreet.

Operation Shamrock

On 27 July 1946 a group of 88 exhausted and bewildered German children arrive by boat at Dún Laoghaire, County Dublin and are brought in trucks to an old British Army barracks at Glencree in the Wicklow mountains. **Operation Shamrock** had begun. It was run by the Irish Red Cross, helped by an Irish group called the Save the German Children Society. Within months 418 German children had arrived, some as young as 3 years. Some had lost their parents in the War and others came from destitute families, with homes lying in rubble. The children were to be kept in foster families and then returned to Germany when it was safe. But for different reasons some stayed and were adopted by new Irish parents.

Lillie Kohlberg was one of those. Her mother and father were killed in the War.

Lillie, aged 8 years, and her twin brother August were brought from an orphanage in Aachen in north Germany to Glencree by Operation Shamrock. Lillie remembers Glencree:

'When I was given soft white bread for my supper together with cocoa made from milk and then given a comfortable bed I thought I was in heaven.'

Sadly, Lillie and August were split up and taken in by different foster parents in Dublin. Much later, August was killed in an accident in South Africa. Lillie was adopted by her foster parents and as an adult she married an Irishman, Jack O'Gorman, and they had 'five fine Irish children'.

About 50 German children stayed in Ireland. You will find a fountain at St Stephen's Green in Dublin, marking Germany's thanks to the Irish for Operation Shamrock.

👉 Lillie Kohlberg, aged 8, the day she was handed over to her Irish foster parents.

👉 This picture from the Irish Press, 23 November 1946, shows German children at Glencree, learning how to handle a hurley stick.

German Children Happy at Glencree

FRANCE AND INDIA BACK SOVIET PLE[A]

(REUTER, UNITED PRESS)

FRANCE and India backed the Soviet motion c[alling on] the Allied Powers to reveal the strength of the[ir forces] in foreign countries, when the United Nations [security] committee resumed its discussion in New Y[ork last] night.

Saying he did not think it possible to link [this] question with disarmament, as Mr. Bevin had su[ggested,] M. Parodi declared for France: "We should retain [it as] constructive in the Soviet proposal and not bury i[t in the] wider problem of disarmament."

Mrs. Vijaya Lakshmi Pandit, head of the Indian delegation, saying she would support M. Molotov's proposal, added that she was "glad the scope of the resolution had been extended to cover former enemy as well as non-enemy territories."

There was no reason why information regarding disposition of troops and location of air and naval bases should not be furnished, she said.

Mr. Noel-Baker (Great Britain), referring to M. Parodi's speech,

in the territory of a sma[ll nation] in time of peace.

"No one can deny tha[t the pres]ence of foreign troops [always] brings pressure to bea[r on the] internal situation."

There were other c[ases, he] said, including the [troops] going on between the [United] States and Iceland.

Troops in territories [that are] members of the Unite[d Nations] had no ground to remai[n, and if] they remained, there mus[t be good] reasons and these [...]

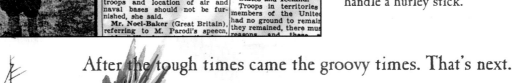

After the tough times came the groovy times. That's next.

Rock 'n' Roll

1950–1960

Our story moves into the 1950s and the groovy 1960s.

Just imagine

You are 10 years old and you are standing on the road outside your house. Loads of other people are there too, all excited, looking up into the night sky, pointing. Waiting. Hoping. Then, yes, there it is! You're the first to see it. 'There … there … look! … there it is!'

It is 5 October 1957. The day before, the world's first man-made satellite was launched by the USSR (Russia). **Sputnik**, they called it, meaning 'fellow traveller'. Sputnik was orbiting the earth, sending back radio signals, a little 'star' moving through outer space. The space age had begun.

It's a dog's life

Then came Sputnik 2, only a few weeks later on 2 November 1957. This time there was a **dog** on board. She had a name, **Laika**, meaning 'barker'. Many people were angry at the idea of Laika being used as an experiment to die in space. And we now know that she died after only about 7 hours from overheating and stress. But Laika has her proud place in history: the first living creature in space, paving the way for humans.

Russia had the first man in space, **Yuri Gagarin** (1961) and the first woman, **Valentina Tereshkova** (1963).

Tough times

The 1950s were tough times in our story of Ireland. More and more people emigrated to England looking for work. The population of the Republic dropped to its lowest-ever point in 1961 with around 2,800,000 people. It was different in Northern Ireland where the population steadily rose.

Women still weren't paid the same as men and married women couldn't work in many jobs. It was also a time of 'censorship', meaning many books and films were banned for having too much violence, sex or the 'wrong' ideas.

The Swingin' Sixties

The sixties started with RTÉ making its first television broadcast on New Year's Eve 1961. The Irish Government began to bring in foreign businesses to give jobs and start the slow build-up of industry which the South had always needed. Hope returned.

There were huge crowds and great pride when Irish-American President **John F Kennedy** (see photo), a direct descendant of Irish famine emigrants, came to Ireland in June 1963. He met Ireland's President Eamon de Valera, spoke in Dáil Éireann and visited the Kennedy home in County Wexford.

The Swingin' Sixties were in, in style! **The Beatles**, from Liverpool, came to Dublin and crossed the world with the songs of the Sixties: 'Love Me Do', 'A Hard Day's Night', 'Help!', 'Yesterday' ... Beatlemania!

Rock 'n' roll

In the 1960s, rock 'n' roll hit the world by storm. A man from Mississippi, USA, had a heart-throbbing hit record called 'Heartbreak Hotel' in 1956. He went on to become one of the biggest music sensations of all time, selling more than a **billion** music records during his life. His name was **Elvis Presley** (right). Elvis gave young people the music to rebel against an older world.

Next ... moonwalking!

Reaching for the Moon

20 July 1969. That was the day man first walked on the moon. When Apollo 11 landed and two American astronauts Neil Armstrong and Edwin 'Buzz' Aldrin jumped onto the lunar surface, Neil Armstrong said: 'That's one small step for Man, one giant leap for Mankind.'

This time Irish people weren't outside looking up but inside watching these truly historic and memorable events on their (black and white) televisions. Mind you, not much more than half the Republic's homes had television sets then.

Did you know ... during the 1960s ...

For the first time the Republic's population began rising. About 4 million people lived on the whole island. That was still **over a million less than 100 years earlier!**

It was US President John F Kennedy who set the target of landing a man on the moon by the end of the 1960s. Sadly, he never saw it happen. President Kennedy had been assassinated in Texas in November 1963, just five months after his visit to Ireland.

The 1960s saw men reaching for the Moon. Neil Armstrong took this photograph of fellow astronaut, Buzz Aldrin, on the lunar landscape.

Skyhigh!

Big numbers of Irish workers built America's skyscrapers and Britain's roads during the first half of the 20th century. The money was good but life was tough.

By the 1960s eight **American Presidents** claimed Irish ancestry, mostly Ulster Presbyterian. Remember Walt Disney, creator of **'Mickey Mouse'**? He had connections to County Kilkenny. As men and women had emigrated they married and grew strong Irish communities ... sending home money and fancy things ... spreading Irish music, dance and, of course, **St Patrick's Day** parades. The biggest parade was in New York City. And the shortest today? That's claimed by Bridge Street, Hot Springs, Arkansas. It's 29.87 metres (almost 98 feet) long, and was once called the 'world's shortest street' in everyday use.

Did you know?

In the United States **35–40 million** people claim some Irish ancestry. Around the world about 70 million people have Irish family roots. Many Protestant-Irish emigrated to Canada and other British Colonies. Between 1801 and 1921 about 8 million Irish men, women and children left Ireland permanently. The most 'Irish' country outside Ireland is Australia.

KISS ME, I'M IRISH!

North and South – a time of hope

By the 1960s, conflict and fighting in Ireland seemed to be over. Ireland as a whole was not united as many had hoped. This left many Roman Catholics (nationalists) in Northern Ireland disappointed. Some felt betrayed by leaders in Dublin. But the island, North and South, appeared to be stable and confident.

In many ways the North was better off. Since the end of the Second World War it had more modern industries, better social welfare payments, a full and free health system and free schooling with free books and meals.

When free secondary education started in the Republic in the 1960s this made a huge difference. It meant better jobs, especially when the Taoiseach Seán Lemass began inviting in modern foreign industries. Seán Lemass also had a more modern approach to Ireland's divisions, as had Northern Ireland's new Prime Minister Terence O'Neill. When both men met for the first time in 1965, many people saw a hopeful future for the island.

☞ Many people took to the streets to protest for civil rights in Derry in 1968.

'I have a dream that my four little children will one day live in a nation where they will not be judged by the colour of their skin but by the content of their character.'

Famous speech by **Martin Luther King**, Washington 1963. King was assassinated in Memphis, Tennessee in 1968. His movement was copied by the **Northern Ireland Civil Rights Association**, seeking equal rights for Catholics.

Sideburns, mini-skirts ….

Young people had other things to think about anyway! Music, fashion, travel and so much else seemed to be changing in exciting ways. Mini-skirts were the rage. The 'fellas' took to sideburns … streak of hair down the side of the face … (lovely) … cheap package holidays to Spain and Greece … (lashing on the sizzling tan oil) … dancing to The Dixies or The Big 8 in the many ballrooms … made the 'swingin sixties' a very different time **… and protests.** It was also a time of protest. In America **Rev. Martin Luther King** led huge marches demanding Civil Rights for black people. Paris witnessed violent student street riots in 1968. Irish women demanded full rights in jobs, politics and birth control. But they had to wait! … until 1973 for equal pay with men … until 1979 for the Republic's first-ever woman government Minister (**Máire Geoghegan-Quinn**). The **Council for the Status of Women** was set up to make sure women got equality.

☞ While people were 'swingin'' in America and Britain in the 1960s, Ireland's showbands were all the rage, with over 400 dance halls around the country such as this one, the Arcadia, in Bray, County Wicklow. Here the Miami showband are performing 'Simple Simon Says' in 1968.

1950s

1960s

1970s

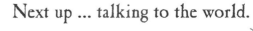

Next up … talking to the world.

A Whole New World

Just imagine Ireland of the 1970s, without mobile phones, computers or the internet but where technology was opening up a whole new world!

Remember how Irish people watched Neil Armstrong walk on the moon on their black and white televisions. That's how they saw Martin Luther King's famous speeches, the Paris riots and all that new fashion. RTÉ television was making a really big impact, especially Gay Byrne on 'The Late Late Show', which started in 1962 and was still going 10 years later (even 40 years later). Colour television began in the USA in 1953, but didn't come to the BBC until 1966 and RTÉ until 1969.

The telephone was invented way back in 1876 but Dublin only got its first international telephone exchange in 1974. Even then, you couldn't ring your Auntie Mary in Australia direct. You had to wait to be connected by telephone operators to exchanges around the world. TV video tape recorders (VTR) arrived in Irish shops from 1975, but the first one was sold in America back in 1956 for $50,000! The internet was invented in 1969, but Irish people had no internet during the 1970s or even the 1980s.

When Telefís Éireann went on air in 1961, Ireland was exposed to culture from around the world, especially from America.

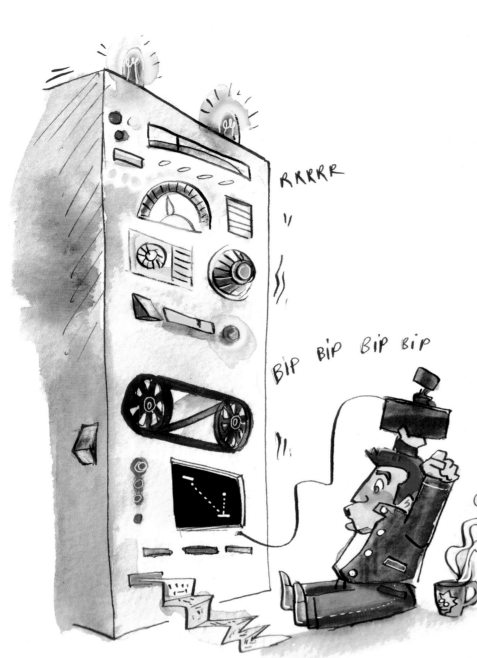

RRRRR

BIP BIP BIP BIP

4,925,000

Ireland
~ population

1981

Growing ... growing ...

The Republic's population kept growing. By 1981 almost 3 million lived there, with around 4,925,000 living on the whole island. And the world's population had reached more than 4 billion!

Next ... they call it 'The Troubles', but it was much more than that.

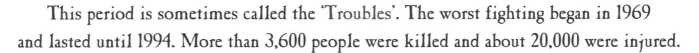

Fighting & Peace

This period is sometimes called the 'Troubles'. The worst fighting began in 1969 and lasted until 1994. More than 3,600 people were killed and about 20,000 were injured.

The 'Troubles'

Many nationalists (mainly Roman Catholics) in Northern Ireland felt that they had not been getting fair play from the Government in Belfast, run by the Ulster Unionists (mainly Protestants). For most Catholics their complaints were about 'civil rights', meaning they wanted equal treatment in jobs, housing and voting in elections. They started a Civil Rights Association and organised street marches.

One of their most important leaders was **John Hume**, from Derry City.

Some Protestant leaders like **Ian Paisley**, a clergyman from Ballymena in County Antrim, tried

to prevent change, saying that what the Civil Rights marchers really wanted was a United Ireland. Ian Paisley and other Unionists wanted Northern Ireland to stay British. A lot of Catholics were forced to leave their homes, especially in Belfast. British soldiers were sent in to bring order but the trouble continued. The **IRA** (Irish Republican Army) started a bombing campaign, killing soldiers, policemen and ordinary people. The IRA wanted a United Ireland and an end to British rule of Northern Ireland. Loyalist (Protestant) groups were also formed to fight and they killed many ordinary Catholics.

The worst year, 1972

That year almost 500 people died, many of them by IRA bombs. Sunday 30 January became known as **'Bloody Sunday'** when British soldiers killed 13 people in Derry City.

Too much happened during the 'Troubles' to tell it all. A lot of people are still sad and hurt. What we can say is that over those terrible years many attempts were made to find peace.

We can say peace began in 1994 when the IRA called a ceasefire and loyalist (Protestant) groups did the same. Most of the violence and fighting stopped. Later, leaders from different political parties and from the Irish and British Governments began a long period of 'round table' talks in Belfast, which lasted two years. A lot of help was given by American President **Bill Clinton**.

☞ People coming up against the British army, Bloody Sunday, Derry, 1972.

Good Friday Agreement

Finally they made an agreement, on Good Friday, 10 April 1998. This became known as the **Good Friday Agreement**.

The Good Friday Agreement was very important. Firstly, it was signed by the British Prime Minister **Tony Blair** and the Irish Taoiseach **Bertie Ahern** and brought their two countries even closer together.

Most importantly, it was an agreement between unionist leaders like **David Trimble** and nationalist leaders like **John Hume** and **Gerry Adams**. This meant people on both sides agreed to live as equals by sharing in the running of Northern Ireland. There were also new links between Northern Ireland and the Republic. The Agreement became even stronger when most people North and South voted for it.

Talking not fighting. Deputy First Minister, Sinn Féin's Martin McGuinness, Taoiseach Bertie Ahern, British Prime Minister Tony Blair, Northern Ireland Secretary Peter Hain and First Minister of the new Government Ian Paisley share a joke at Stormont Buildings in Belfast, May 2007.

Hope and trouble

The Good Friday Agreement brought both hope and trouble. It took several years for the IRA to destroy their weapons and for many unionists to accept the Agreement.

A day to remember

Then came a really wonderful day: 8 May 2007, the day peace was really secured. At Stormont Buildings, Belfast, a new government for Northern Ireland began. Its leaders were Ian Paisley, unionist, and Martin McGuinness, nationalist. Northern Ireland's children could now look forward to a much happier future.

Next up ... Jack's Army and the Celtic Tiger.

The Celtic Tiger

On now to a brighter future.

Ireland's story began to get better and better

The 1990s were a bit like the Swingin' Sixties, especially in the Republic of Ireland. Mary Robinson was elected Ireland's first woman President in 1990. That was very new. 'Riverdance', the musical, hit the world. Irish music was suddenly 'cool'. Dublin city was buzzing with young people and new faces from different countries. Ireland was making a big mark. People called it the Celtic Tiger.

A journey of hope

Ireland's new journey really began back in 1973 when the Republic and Northern Ireland joined the European Union (then called the European Economic Community). Irish people became part of a wonderful peace project where countries came together in peace instead of fighting wars.

European money helped the country greatly. Farmers improved their farms and sold their products at good prices in many countries. Dublin got a fine new electric railway, the Dublin Area Rapid Transport (DART).

Still, it was a long time before Ireland 'took off'. In fact the 1980s were tough times for many people. Ireland still had a lot of poor people. In 1985 there were about 220,000 people unemployed. Too many had to emigrate to find jobs.

Jack's army

One thing did 'take off' at this time, **Jack's Army**. Jack's Army was made up of thousands of madly waving football supporters, dressed in green, singing Olé Olé Olé! They followed the Republic of Ireland's football team which reached two big international Championship for the first time ever: the European final in 1988 and the World Cup in 1990. Jack's Army was named after the team's manager, an Englishman called **Jack Charlton**.

Do you know what's gone?

Ireland's **railways** were disappearing fast as more and more people got cars. The island of Ireland had almost 5,600 kilometres (3,500 miles) of railway track in 1920 but only about 2,400 (1,500 miles) in 1980. That's 3,200 kilometres (2,000 miles) of railway track gone! Ireland's **farmers** were also 'disappearing'. In 1973 the Republic had about 230,000 farmers. In 1999 there were 144,000. That's 86,000 farmers gone!

The DART at Pearse Station, Dublin.

The Celtic Tiger marches on

At the end of the 1990s, the 'Celtic Tiger' was roaring. By then the Republic had received about 50 billion euro from the European Union. New roads were built and the country was much improved. The 'Celtic Tiger' became important for making high technology gadgets and computers. More and more Irish people, who had emigrated earlier, returned home to get new jobs. Many foreign people arrived too. Agriculture was not as important though. Ireland's population rose and rose especially in towns and cities. By the end of the 1990s the Republic reached a new high of about 3,900,000 people and Northern Ireland around 1,700,000. So on the whole island? Yes, 5,600,000. And the world's population? 6 billion!

5,600,000.
Ireland
~population

Bob's aid

On 13 July 1985 an Irish singer **Bob Geldof** organised two amazing **Live Aid** rock concerts, in London and Philadelphia USA, to help starving people in Ethiopia. Live Aid was televised around the world and people donated $60 million. Even still, more than a million Ethiopian children and adults died of starvation.

Next ... into a new millennium!

Remember that lush, beautiful island of 9,000 years ago, where nobody lived?
Look at it now. So different.

A lively land

As we travel through a new millennium, Ireland is a growing, changing land. The island's children all seem to have a mobile phone. **Peace** is all around – and hope. Politicians are working together in Northern Ireland's new government. The **euro** has come in to the Republic. Belfast is getting better all the time with new houses, more jobs and a fine waterfront. Dublin gets a tall, pointy **Spire** and a **LUAS** tram system. World poverty is not forgotten. In 2005, after another global music show, Bob Geldof and Bono get promises of help – $50 billion from the richer countries.

New century top stuff

As the new century began, in the Republic 537,000 homes had the **internet**.

2,398,769 tonnes of **rubbish** was collected. Yuk!

People from faraway places like Nigeria, Poland, Brazil and China have come to work and live in Ireland. More than 400,000 people on the island were born abroad.

The top ten names

Sean   Jack   Conor   Adam   James   Daniel   Cian   Luke   Michael   Aaron

Emma   Katie   Sarah   Amy   Aoife   Ciara   Sophie   Chloe   Leah   Niamh

... and the island's population?
ALMOST 6 MILLION ... and rising!

6,000,000

Ireland population

About 20 million people a year travelled through Dublin Airport, 3 million through Shannon. Belfast Airport was renamed '**George Best Belfast City Airport**'. Cork, Derry, Knock, Kerry, Waterford, Sligo, Donegal and Galway now had airports.

THE END ... not really.

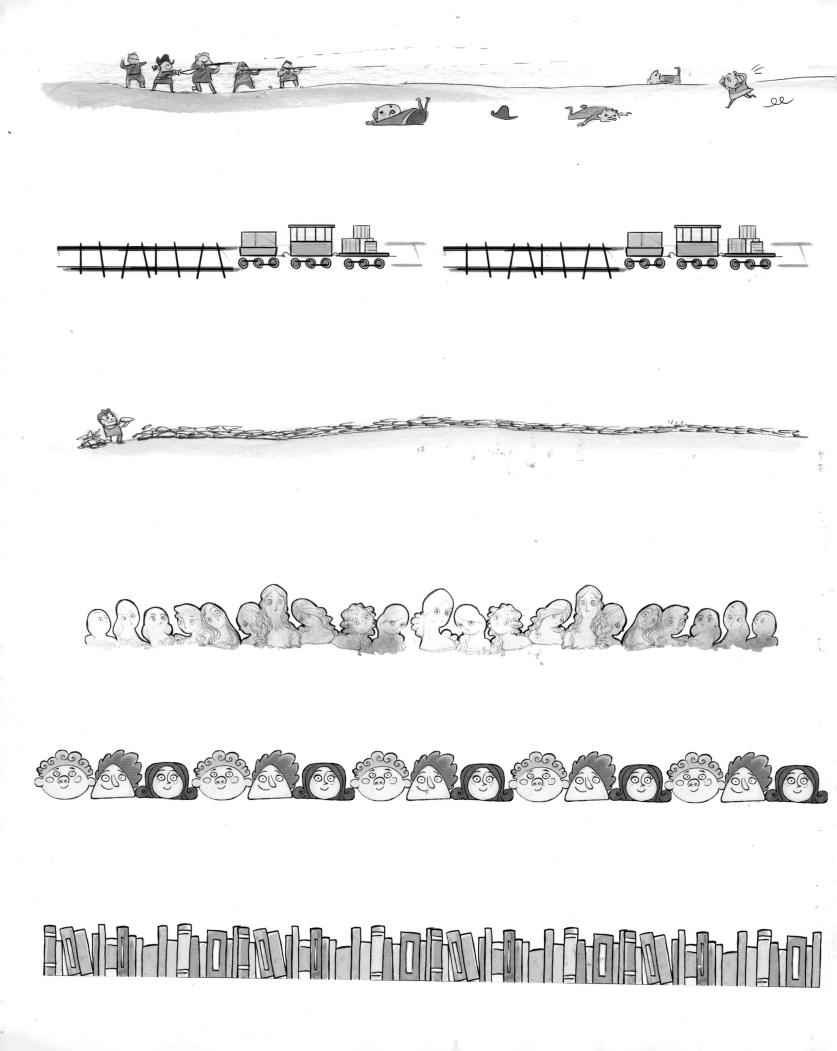